True Savage 7

Chris Green

Lock Down Publications and Ca$h Presents

True Savage 7

A Novel by *Chris Green*

Chris Green

Lock Down Publications
P.O. Box 944
Stockbridge, Ga 30281

Visit our website @
www.lockdownpublications.com

Lock Down Publications
Like our page on Facebook: Lock Down Publications @
www.facebook.com/lockdownpublications.ldp
Cover design and layout by: **Dynasty Cover Me**
Book interior design by: **Shawn Walker**
Edited by: **Jill Alicea**

Stay Connected with Us!

Text **LOCKDOWN** to 22828 to stay up-to-date with new re-
leases, sneak peaks, contests and more…
Thank you.

Submission Guideline.

Submit the first three chapters of your completed manuscript to ldpsubmissions@gmail.com, subject line: Your book's title. The manuscript must be in a .doc file and sent as an attachment. Document should be in Times New Roman, double spaced and in size 12 font. Also, provide your synopsis and full contact information. If sending multiple submissions, they must each be in a separate email.

Have a story but no way to send it electronically? You can still submit to LDP/Ca$h Presents. Send in the first three chapters, written or typed, of your completed manuscript to:

LDP: Submissions Dept
P.O. Box 944
Stockbridge, Ga 30281

DO NOT send original manuscript. Must be a duplicate.

Provide your synopsis and a cover letter containing your full contact information.

Thanks for considering LDP and Ca$h Presents.

Dedication:

Cerenity Armoni Massiyah Green my heartbeat, the blessing from Allah, and my stubborn, beautiful Baby mother Reshonda Evans. Your growth has risen, princess. You are a true genius, and I'm so grateful to have a daughter as precious and brilliant-minded as yourself. Daddy will protect and provide for you for eternity. You are the reason I work, and you can always have every single piece of whatever your daddy owns. I love you, baby. The world is yours when I get home. It's coming, so stay strong and smiling like always.

Chris Green

Acknowledgements

10:21a.m., Friday morning, July 24, 2020, I was sitting in my brother's room beating the keys down on a book that I cried, bled, cursed, and doubted so many different times, a book that I felt should have gave me a blast-off position in the literary realm. The mouth-dropping series has six pieces that have been on Amazon for two years now. The seventh was placed on hold for years all because I felt the special vision I wrote wasn't presented to its full potential. This series goes so deep that you literally could slice a boulder in half with one page of its action-packed drama. I wanna thank my boss man for creating this journey and filling me in on so much priceless knowledge. You are a tough coach that a player would have to bear large patience and understanding with. Your tough but honest answers to these mysterious problems I experienced were a stepping stone for me to practice a way to cut that nasty habit out of my course. Thank you, big bro. LDP has raised me into a soldier, and I'm honored to keep delivering these banging street novels for the company.

My momma, Dolsellia…I'm taking care of you and Cerenity when I'm released from behind this caged world of destruction. You gave up so much to see me grow and win, from birth until the moment that is ticking on earth at this very second. You've held an irreplaceable love that no one has given me, and I thank you, Queen. You're my everything along with Cerenity. Your wishes are my command when I'm released. Shout out to the Gang: Big Osa traditional ©70023rd ties15 12 OsaLove4DaAnimalPak; Carl Mccline (C.j); Charles Cary (Drop); Nate Nation; Razziq (Saint; Qawi; Rip Sip; Rip Barry Mathis; my best hater, but first supporter, Kevin Green, my right hand every day, the one that can teach a chump to get understandings sweeter than easy and freeze! Start with reverting back and conquer the meaning of what the simple, but complicated word UNDERSTAND before acting.

Deangelo Green, my reflection. Blood brother, same mother. My replica and side angel through any war the one who would go against the world about me. Love ya, big bro. I'm almost home. Stay growing, gaining, and grinding. I'll be beside you in a few wake-ups. My brother Timothy Johnson. Love ya to death. The motivators and supporters who've shown up and lent a hand through my incarceration. I'm shooting for the stars with business ventures and I can mentally feel the winning line approaching. I will be the greatest and most diverse author, rapper, poet, comedian, and most loyal friend, someone people can vouch positively about. Don't say I didn't try to include the ones who denied my request with being a part of my success. We all have journeys and congratulate each other on gains, whenever they're recognized. Pray for change. Offer Dua for hardships. Keep Allah first. My favorite fan Feather Harrison has been on Ghost's bumper for a while, and I'm greatly relieved that she is satisfied (Myridah Helene Young).

Shout outs to DAbabezzzLana! DelanaThewriter and her twin Kenzie. I'm trying to build, and you always show me a vision that no other has given. Hopefully it's Blessed upon me. Love you. Shouts for Charmaine Jackson (my Facebook mama LOL!)

Shouts for the trooper and the bull of being the toughest JAW LOCK respect checker: Destiny Skai, of course! LOL!

All the other first row supporters, I love y'all: Jane, Shawn, Janice, Alexus, my big bro Marius Clark, the whole Green family, my aunts Melita and Candice, my sister Shanika, my cousin Michelle, my grandma Dianna, and Great-granny Doris; Khloe, Tina, Kayla, Kristina, Valerie, Sam,

Devin, Neicey, and Miyanna. You all are my lifeline .I got y'all for life. My twin brudda Drewski #1992 July...Rip Capo Nuke. And everyone else who's just too long to mention, just know that y'all always will be able to have me first at your side if need be. May Allah reward you all with blessings, and Asalamu laikum to all my great Muslim brothers, whom I cherish...WeRBooks! Author Chris Green:

Instagram: Iamkosa_
Facebook: Author Chris Green

All donations from my true supporters towards the lawyer's petition regarding my parole and release on gaining my freedom are to be sent to my mother, Dolsellia Green, along with your full name and phone number The push for my growth has been sheltered long enough, and now I'm pushing for the gates to open where I can travel the world with this same talent my fans love so much. Tons of family and dear friends have made a way to starting the word for this movement, and I'm grateful. I hope that soon we will reach the goal with flying colors.

To all: stay safe, positive, and blessed. This is *True Savage 7*.You are very welcome, and be sure to leave your review on Amazon as to what you all predicted for the Grey Family. Thank you and enjoy.

My awesome catalog of novels is located on Amazon and Barnes and Nobles.com, or check your nearest Walmart.
True Savage 1-7
Midnight Cartel 1-3
Dope Boy Magic 1-3
City of Kingz 1-2
Married to a Boss, But Pregnant by My Rx ft. Destiny Skai 1-3

*Coming soon: the biggest tears you'll ever shed for my first urban dramatic, poetic novel? I will tell you soon LOL.

*_City of Kingz 3: The Mafia's Payback_

*_Black Snow, Crumbs to Bricks_

*_Dopeboy Magic 4: The Collision of a Certified Dopegirl_

*_Spoiled Bananas_ - This is Jamrock collab with a surprise co-author (Inshallah)

The lit action and comedy-packed series:

Lucky Lola and _Seven 1 and 2_

WHAT Y'ALL THINK ABOUT _TRUE SAVAGE: THE MOVIE?_

Chris Green

Chapter 1
Flashback: Ten years ago...

The loud thunderstorm that banged through Ghost's eardrums forced him to crack his eyelids out of the coma-like trance he was in. The wretched pain that was streaming through the side of his head forced him to wince lightly. He placed a finger on the swollen scar that rested under his right temple and rubbed it, following the deep trail that led to the center of his neck. The thought of getting caught slipping sat in quickly and reality finally snapped him out of the dazed trance, making him reach at his hip for the strap. He jumped up and looked around the dark-ass room. A small light shone from the far eastern window, and a large man dressed in a black sweat suit occupied a wide desk in front of him. He was facing the opposite way, and nothing in Ghost's eyesight was visible to use as a weapon in case he played as the opposition.

The rain was tapping gently against the window and before Ghost could take another breath, the seated man spoke.

"I cleaned your gun. It's sitting in the chair to your right along with your clothes." His attention was still occupied at the desk and whatever he had in his hands.

Ghost's eyes shifted to the rolling chair, where his gun sat on top of his outfit.

"It's not loaded," the man said, rotating around slowly and hitting the switch above his head.

The light blurred Ghost's vision slightly, but the huge creepy cop man sitting twenty feet away from him couldn't be missed. His grey box cut was shaped up neatly, and his brown eyes were stiffer than a mountain rock. The appearance of his clothing screamed ex-military or Cuban cocaine boss. His arms were big as fuck. The huge guy was sitting down, but you could still tell that he was nearly seven foot tall. The calm face was emotionless with no trail of tiny passion leaves to sweep along the path. He hadn't blinked, flinched, or given any sign that he was worried about the mental nut case that was standing in front of him.

"Who the fuck are you? And I swear I'm leaving out this bitch if this has anything to do with attempting to kill me." Ghost pointed with a look of death in his dilating pupils of rage.

"I'm not the man you need to be worried about, son," he replied before taking a sip of a glass of beer to his side. "Those Italians nearly killed you, and if I wouldn't have gotten to you in time, I wouldn't have to feel like I'm forced to give you a heartbreaking and fraudulent lie. I prefer the truth, and was designed to implement nothing different," the veteran mercenary explained with no care for Ghost's choices. Any severe movement would cause him to use force.

"Your reason sounds beyond exceptional, but I don't even trust the words from my own flesh and blood. Spill that shit, 'cause we both stuck. I feel like you deserve a fucking Oscar for this explanation." His tone thickened to ensure that nervousness was the last thing crossing his mind. The sharp pain that quaked in his body had him breathing harshly, and the large gunshot wound in his shoulder was bandaged tighter than a deadbolt lock.

The mysterious murderer in his presence crossed his leg with a long sigh, expressing the patience he was trying to exercise. "Your father placed a call for my help, and I assisted. It seems that whoever is after you placed a large block of hatred in Michael's heart for them, and you too. He warned you of a disaster waiting to happen before you left the comfort of your island, and you didn't listen. His granddaughters, the family, and other workers who placed their lives on the line for the business were his duty to protect by any means. The time he lost away from his own happiness was a pain he refused to relive again after it was finally given back when your family reunited. He's not taking the chances on their blood being spilled because you continue to engage in a war that will never cease. The Ramirez family has suffered at your hands, and he's willing to remove you if that will allow the suffering of his bloodline to end. He's alerted me with a message for you, and his promise for standing behind the statement is one that I'm willing to put my mother's life on the line. He will make it reality if provoked or forced. He's ordering your death on sight if anyone is aware of your return, or if his mind suspects you are pondering or attempting any option besides the ones explained. He's gonna hunt you down until your last breath is taken." The man tilted his head with a nod like the request was smooth and acceptable.

Ghost laughed to himself before folding his arms with a disbelieving attitude. The love for his two Queens and his children was a major factor that he was willing to die about with no questions.

Michael had a fucked-up mind. The two decades he spent inside of his grandfather's basement had to be surely eating at his brain, but there was nothing that a bullet to the skull couldn't fix.

"My father has no authority over me, and I clearly explained that I was willing to handle all affairs without any trouble on my own. The shit my family possesses and holds power over is established and built off me alone. Not him. My work…my home…my kids." Ghost licked his lips like the talk was making him crave blood. "I'm willing to take my chances." His lips frowned with distaste.

The threat and disagreement for the warning forced the room to grow silent. A vicious boom of thunder erupted between the moments of silence.

The lunatic assassin sat up straighter than a bold base line for the letter L, swallowing his spit with a sympathetic face. He huffed with pity, "May your soul be granted mercy, and relief. Michael will be the last thing you see if paths between you two happen to cross. It's the best advice you'll ever hear. If you stay away for a while to form an end to this shitty calamity that's causing troubles for your family, it'll allow you to handle your problem. Leave your father for the last death on your list. He's not gonna change his mind."

Ghost let the serious remark soak deeply into his brain waves. Ghost knew that Michael's words were literally serious. The nuts of actually trying the stunt was a shock, but the fight with his heartless and bloody mind was a warning he refused to sleep on. The passion for claiming a life with Michael was like the love a bumblebee shared for the summer heat and bundled roses embedded with canary yellow pollen. The thought of Erica and Tiffany sent a wave of painful and pulsating thumps through his skull. The deceitful plot that his father was implementing was more than just a lesson from a parent. He was trying to dish out the same torture and pain he received from his Father Jesus, the God of Cocaine and also the legendary leader at the table for the ruthless and wealthy Ramirez bloodline. A person who couldn't control a double-minded attitude was dangerous when pondering something that was desired. The pain he thought about Michael preparing to enforce on his girls wasn't about to be out of love and protection. It was revenge and hatred for the protection that he failed to provide for his own soulmates and children. He didn't respect the man Ghost became without his presence being available. He admired the perfection that was grounded with his Queens and craved the same power and feeling. The way that Erica and Tiffany were obedient to his every desire and command. That precious time they spent with the children, and also the need to fulfill their every desire as a parent. That passionate feeling was removed from him the day his father Jesus decided to throw him into captivity for eternity. The reputation his son engraved through the grounds of Atlanta had situated his family well with the finances, which he was preparing to seize control of, and the will to declare his throne back for the King was officially being presented. The feeling was so addictive that he was even willing to be the death of his own son to feel the sweet life he possessed.

"Who are you? And if you claim to not have any dealings with my father's dirty and treacherous ties, I wanna know how to stop him. You the motherfucking key card to do it," Ghost demanded with a look that said the shit was chiseled in stone with no hopes of reconstructing anything different from that.

The Beast rose to his feet and released the pressure with a menacing laugh. His wide and humongous arms started to spread as he flexed his muscles, daring Ghost to try it. The table behind him was finally visible, and two black Springfield 9mm's rested on top. The intense tension rising between them was suffocating the oxygen, but the staring war they shared gave that secret confirmation that only one of them was really leaving that bitch alive.

Ghost was lost as to where he currently stood, but the big man's story started to sound like he was told to do more than just deliver the news. The dark silence was dead in the air, so dead that you could smell Michael's assassin blood flowing quickly within his torso and lower stomach. He was scared as fuck, and Ghost smelt it lingering off his ass like a stench from a sick perverted granddaddy who used that skunk cologne in the sixty's. He was so busy kicking the fearless role that he never noticed the sharp, razor-like utensil in the clutch of Ghost's palm – the same shit he used to remove the soaked bloody shirt and bullet resting inside of his flesh.

Before the thought could leave Ghost's mind, the nigga reached for the pistols on the table behind him. Moving quick on his feet, Ghost rushed the giant idiot, closing their distance in a mere second. Before Mr. Professional could do a full rotation, Ghost was sliding the sharp metal deeply into the back of his neck.

"Arghh!" the man snapped as a giant gash split smoothly apart like a soggy piece of paper. The killer used all of his strength to sling Ghost forcefully off his back and onto the floor. His eyes bulged before he yelled with rage, "You're fucking dead!" He swung a right hand as he jumped hastily back up to his feet.

Ghost was swifter, and the swing was slow as turtle sex. He landed a solid two piece to his right jaw. He slipped and smashed the bow into his rib cage. One wild punch from the man's fist forced a stumble from Ghost. The men were swinging heavy as shit. The small tussle with the two crashed violently over onto the desk table he had recently sat at. They were going hard like two wild bulls in the pen, and the fight for another day of life was past heated in the boxed-in sweat box. The men sweated and wrestled for the guns underneath the access shit on the floor.

The man rammed a fist into Ghost's side. He heaved in pain, but held a strong grip on the motherfucker's right wrist. The sight of his lucky survival knife glistened clearly in his eye. The man's arms were pressing down into his throat to crush his life and continue on with the collecting of the five million dollar bounty that was thumb-tacked to his head.

Feeling the light fade a smidge in his eyes pumped Ghost's adrenaline hard enough to make him reach over to the side of him, and snatch up the thin metal slicer. He rammed it deeply into the man's throat twice. The final blow was rammed through the bottom of his chin, breaking the lodged blade into his head. The weight of his body grew heavier and a thick pool of warm blood began to pour quickly from the severe puncture wounds.

Rolling the dead dummy over to his side, Ghost inhaled a sigh of relief. His heart rate was racing, and the animal he had just taken out had his strength dispersing completely from his body. The nausea dazed him for a second, but the will to live when you had no choice would force you to keep going.

After taking his time to get the fuck up off the floor, Ghost glanced down at his soulless victim. The game had switched drastically in a matter of hours. His father's plot threw a confusing and twisted wrench in the drama, and his mission was quite clear. Now that the truth was uncovered, Ghost was gonna be sure to follow his mind. The enemies who caused the pain would pay first, and once the war against the ops ended, he was gonna head back to the islands and face the dealer of the cards himself. Old problems had to be eliminated, and Eva was the first person to cross his mind. Tony from Italy would surely be getting a personal visit in New York to bury ties with Pauly, and the dirty snakes that made the decision to touch Shadow and Jimmie were gonna be located and deleted also. The demon in him bubbled from the death risk at hand, and once his wicked eyes started to twitch off balance, Ghost psyched his entire brain out for one outcome: to dismember the head of anyone who stood in between his protection and love for the Grey family. Lies were being dished out, and the order to see his demise was starting to be revealed. Weeks back, he got a slight hint when he received word about Eva's ten million dollar bounty on his head for the deaths of her three angels: Romeo, Raphael, and Miguel.

Snatching his clothes from the small rolling chai, he placed them on and checked the chamber of his gun. Rushing over to the messy table area, he picked the two loaded pistols off the floor, including all the extra bullets he had spotted. A Kevlar SWAT vest was dangling on the hook of a wooden coat rack, and he made sure to snatch it on the way towards the basement door. The dead man's car keys were sitting visibly on the counter. The man no longer needed to drive. He was a casualty from the crooked hands of Michael.

The next move in Ghost's mind was clear. He was about to knock on the doors of his ducks one by one until he squashed every soul involved with the tormented plan for his downfall and demise. His mind flashed back to the sign he had received a few weeks ago. The talk around the criminal world was that Eva had the keys to revenge, and the reason people were clawing at the family's artery was the ten million dollar bounty she placed on his head for the deaths of her three seeds of destruction The city was about to be returned as his playground with the treachery and the heartless soul shit he was bringing.

After exiting the room, he made his way en route to the residence of Reeses's caretaker first. A promise was made, and it would be kept, not to mention his own guarantee for the precious girls of his world. The devil was alive, and Ghost was about to prove that horrifying truth to the ones in line to be killed.

Chapter 2
Ghost's Mansion
Virgin Islands, 9:00 a.m.
Two days after the disappearance

It had been over forty-nine hours, and not one call had been made home to ensure his safety and relay the message of what he planned on doing next. Erica knew that his arrogance could get the best of his secluded thinking and help would be the last thing he wanted offered to him. The job on executing her attackers had been in effect for a while, and shit was really starting to fall deeper than she expected. The rumor of him being ambushed at the airport when he arrived in Atlanta was forcing her to worry and think the worst.

Tiffany walked inside the double doors of the bedroom with Laylah following directly behind. Her face showed that she was displeased, and the thought about finding her own damn man was starting to cross her mind. She opened the walk-in closet and grabbed a grey leather padded box from underneath her clothing shelf. She sat in on the bed and cracked the lock. She pulled her gun and passport out. Her eyes rotated and stopped on Erica, who sat motionless at the bedroom window.

"Are we going to look ourselves, or is this feeling gonna keep eating our asses until we snap? Ghost may need our help, Erica." Tiffany's light green eyes stressed the sincerity her heart felt for him.

Erica exhaled, not trying to think for the worst. There was so much bad shit occurring that anything else would literally crack her sane mind frame. Ghost was gonna fix the damn problem and make his way home, the same as he always did. Nothing would break that faith in her mind.

"He's gonna show up, Tiff. Don't create a bad picture over us right now. I can't handle that." She blinked her dark brown eyes, calmly praying for the phone to ring.

The knock on her bedroom door forced her and Tiffany to look back at the same time. Michael was standing in the doorway with a dry expression on his face. A truthful person could never hide shit when it was bad news that no one was prepared to hear. The posture he presented raised Erica's suspicion, and she instantly rose to her feet.

"Michael, is there a problem? What have you heard?" she questioned curiously.

"He's gone." The statement fell from his tongue like that was just the end of the story. Michael's eyes locked in on them and he could see the backlash about to explode at any second.

Erica gasped before shaking Michael's words straight out of her mind. Her shaky hand wiggled as she raised a finger up to him. "What the fuck does gone mean?

Tiffany held the center of her chest, hoping that it meant he was gone from the city and on his way back to the islands. When his reply didn't come quick enough, Erica sniffled lightly before her jaws clenched down tightly.

"I said tell me that it's a fucking joke! Tell me he's coming home. Right now!" she yelled while looking for any sign of agreement from his father.

"I think we need to stay put on the Islands for a while until things calm down. The family is in danger, and I don't want to ever say that I kept faith my entire life just to see all my relatives die off before I got a chance to love and grow with them. I'm sorry, sweetheart." Michael dropped a fake tear of sorrow for the filthy-ass lie he constructed.

Tiffany's eyes were running before the confirmation had a chance to escape his mouth. There was never such a thing as joking about the death of a man who made it possible for their family to be breathing at that exact second. No one could meet that standards of the love he dispersed, and if the slightest doubt came to them as far as trusting in his return, Ghost would have made contact. It was a conquering energy that Tiffany felt since the first time their eyes connected with that shivering glare in his pupils. She never lost that incredible strength and trust until that day.

"Noooo!" Erica screamed while gripping at the sides of her hair tightly. Her legs crumpled, forcing her knees to crash against the floorboard. "Please tell me he's coming back. I've lost too much! Don't take him away from me pleaseee!"

Tiffany immediately jumped down Michael's throat. "Damn, dude, did it seem like a good idea to fuck up our lives with this news and then just sit back calm like this isn't a fucking issue?" Her green eyes pierced his face with hate.

"I warned him," Michael stated with a stern tone. "Now it's obvious that you see he wasn't going to listen to anyone or respect the rules to family safety. It's nothing we can do if the cause was by his own hands, Tiffany. Now I know that you're not prepared to hear this, but things were bound to collapse on him after the bloody trail of destruction he carved inside the hearts of all the competition. War isn't meant to be fought with all enemies just because a person feels their reputation is built from it. I'm here to help protect the rest of this family as much as possible, but that will only work if you girls allow me to step up and make decisions for all instead of self," he offered, knowing that there was only so much help left.

Erica stood slowly to her feet after grasping on to Michael's statement. Her eyes were turning dark red from the painful reality of Ghost being snatched away and after all the past losses she suffered through. Tiffany held her hand gently, trying to ease the rigid pain, but Erica's mind was calculating other feelings after looking into Michael's eyes.

"You're sitting here telling me that my man is gone forever? The father of my children is dead, and the only thing that you seem worried about is family safety?" she questioned with slanted eyes. "The word safety wouldn't even be able to hold weight around here if it wasn't for Ghost. This family business and operation, providing for all the needs for me and Tiffany…that was all given by him. What gives you the fucking idea that you can step up and help us win after my nigga laced the world around our fingers without you? His blood is sacred, but your vibe and emotions show me that you feel another way."

"It was never my intention to make you feel that I came here to pamper you and tell you the shit that love's to be spoken around here. I can't fix myself to lie just to make you, or anyone else in this household, to feel better. I'm here to be honest and change the danger and sloppiness of our actions. Chance was my son, but that doesn't mean he had you or the children's best interests at heart if he continued to place everyone into harm's way." Michael gave her a pitying look from the irrational thinking she was expressing.

Tiffany could see the anger rising in her face, and before she could grab ahold of Erica, her feet were carrying her towards Michael like a bullet. Her nose was nearly touching the space between his eyes and her lips quivered furiously.

"You aren't running shit in my house, and this family isn't allowing blood to be shed without retaliation. I gave up my entire life for the love of my life. I proved that neither the law nor anyone else could compare with the bond we shared for building excellence. I lost my career, my son, and now my husband. I want blood, and that's an order," she hissed with a demonic tone.

Michael glared down into Erica's eyes, knowing that her words were glued in like concrete. Explaining his opinion wouldn't make any difference, and before he made his move-ment to enforce his hand, he decided to let her grieve over his son whichever way she chose.

Taking a step back from her, he turned his head towards Tiffany, holding his granddaughter close to her side. "I sug-gest you calm her before we all have a laser beam on our skulls by morning. We can all shoot for vengeance about Chance, but I would like you girls to remember that we do have kids who must be protected by any cost. That's still my son's bloodline, and I'm willing to die before anyone places them in jeopardy. Be sure to soak that up your fucking head while you're passing out orders!" he shot back before turning to exit the room.

Tiffany was clueless as to what to even say after being hit with the devastating news. Her tears wouldn't cease from fall-ing, and all she could do was stare down at Laylah hugging her waistline with a worried face. There was no understanding or explaining Ghost's death to her, and it was impossible to force a daddy's girl who was his spitting image to believe he would never return.

Erica was so distraught that she literally stood in the same spot for over five minutes. It was a nightmare that she couldn't run from or wake from. The love that kept a firm grip on her disfigured life had now been taken away. There would be no running back to his arms when shit got rough, no more of his touch to ease her pain from the sickening world she despised so much. Life didn't matter without him being present for their family, and her mind could hear the exact words he would be whispering in her ear at the time for comfort: "Never forget that family is first, and we will bargain with no one about our own. No one will love y'all more than me, and there is no op-tion of leaving, whether you agree or not. Be my other half and move with me, until you eventually become just like me."

She remembered his words as if they were a rehearsed movie script. The pure woman that once lived inside of her heart was fading deeply into the shade as a new inner nutcase was being created. Closing her eyes tightly, the last two tears of sorrow were sliced by Erica's backhand. The deep breath she released allowed the dark energy to enter her soul faster than God's will to take a life. Her brown eyes began gazing around the master bedroom awkwardly, and Tiffany could see that her entire body posture had changed. A sinister laugh escaped her lips softly before humming out a sweet tone of insanity.

"Ms. Grey is what you wanted, Ms. Grey is what you got!" Erica mumbled with an evil smile caressing her face.

Tiffany moved over to her side slowly and placed a hand on her shoulder. "I know it sounds hard, Erica, but we are family, and you're not about to go through this on your own. I got you through whatever," she assured with a caring voice.

Erica's neck turned in a creepy motion until their faces were spaced a few inches away from each other. A wry smile formed before she spoke. "You know that no one can love you more than me, right?"

Her statement caused a slight shiver to flow down the center of Tiffany's back. Not only were Erica's eyes piercing through her like fresh metal against the cold flesh of a dead corpse, but it sounded as if Ghost was speaking directly through her at the moment. It was a promise that he never broke, and also a remark that he always enforced when shit was about to spiral out of control. Erica was waiting for an answer, and the small twitch in her right eye gave the indication of only wanting the correct one.

"Yes, I know that." Tiffany nodded.

"Good." She leaned forward kissing her lips gently. "Never forget that," Erica added before walking out of their bedroom.

Tiffany was confused about her statement, but she knew one thing for sure. The delicate flower that once circulated around the heart of Erica was replaced with a ring of fire. She was never gonna be the same after that day, and that was only a minor figure of speech for what was next to fall upon the Grey family.

Chris Green

Chapter 3
Virgin Islands
Ten years later

The small yellow cab that pulled in front of the Grey's mansion came to a slow halt once it reached the top of its hill. The sun shining across the beach water could be seen from the front of the luxurious home. A few seagulls could be spotted flying through the air, and a whiff of death could be smelt every time a small wave brushed against the sand on the secluded property. The old Jamaican taxi owner glanced back at the man in his back seat with a look of worry.

"Are yu sure dis is da rite place, mon? No one is allowed on the Grey family's territory."

"Sounds great. This must be the spot I'm looking for," he replied sarcastically before stepping out.

The taxi driver wasted no time smashing his gas pedal, leaving a cloud of white smoke in the air. The visitor waved a hand, trying to clear his vision, and once the scene was visible, he stood face to face with a large black gate. It was slightly cracked, giving the impression to enter at your own risk, and a few cars could be seen parked, facing towards their front door.

Huffing lightly, he walked through the guarded driveway, and spotted over ten armed men within his first four steps. Their faces were covered with a half mask, and their body movements were stiffer than a group of mannequins. It almost could go for a wax museum if their eyes weren't blinking with every inch he proceeded inside.

"Wah gwan?" one of the Rastafarians mumbled while tilting his head.

Instead of giving them any reaction, he kept it pushing until he reached the front door of the massive home. The mahogany wood double doors were standing nearly fifteen feet tall, and a dead silence fell over the parking lot before the guards locked and secured the fence through which he entered. Looking behind him, he noticed that the group of dread heads were now surrounding the exit until further notice.

Shrugging his shoulders, he placed his attention back on the doors in front of him and rang the doorbell twice. Of course it felt awkward to have a team of crazy Jamaicans, posted behind him with assault rifles, but he needed assurance that his mission wasn't in vain before he shot it out with the live wires, who obviously felt he was trespassing.

The sound of the front door opening forced his heart to speed up.

Erica stepped from behind the door with her beautiful black hair laying down past her shoulders. A silk form-fitting Gucci dress was hugging her curves gently, and her feet were slid inside a pair of Gucci fur flip flops. A black nine millimeter pistol hung down by her right side, and a cell phone was in the other hand, engaging into the conversation on her line at the moment. Once she locked eyes with the man in front of her, she dropped the gun and the phone covering her mouth. Sharp tears formed at the edge of her eyelids thinking that her mind was playing tricks on her, but that wasn't the case. "Shadow?" she whimpered lightly.

Removing his shades, he exhaled a sigh of relief before nodding silently.

Jumping in his arms. Erica latched on to his neck tighter than a child who hadn't seen her parents since birth. Her tears began to pour into his chest, and the sound of her cries forced Tiffany to rush out of the front door. The moment she spotted

Erica and Shadow embracing, a large chill maneuvered through her body.

"Shadow, is that you?"

"Hey Sis." He smiled, still holding Erica in his arms.

Tiffany wasted no time rushing over to join their family moment and embrace a man who she truly considered to be her brother. He was the only thing close enough to Ghost that cared dearly for the family, and after ten long years, he was back.

"We thought you were dead." Erica leaned up to get a better look at him.

"I kind of figured that after I gained my right mind back. The last thing I remember was heading for New York to look for you. I was hoping to find you alive, and ended up falling into my own damn mix-up. Where is Ghost?" Shadow looked back and forth between the two women for the brother would destroy the world for.

Tiffany lowered her vision for a slight second before looking up into his blue eyes. "Ghost is gone Shadow."

His face twisted into a ball of anger from her response, but he didn't react without viewing Erica's posture. Her stern face was on, but her dark brown eyes always gave away the pain she was truly feeling inside. He could tell that there was more to the story, but the shit he just heard wasn't about to be accepted, period. "What do you mean gone, Tiffany?" he asked with a look of disbelief.

Erica placed a hand on his shoulder and sighed. "Ghost has been dead for ten years, Shadow. He left for Atlanta in search of Bernard's killer, and never made it back."

"What do you mean Bernard's killer? Where is my nephew? What the hell is going on?" His white skin began to flush bright red.

Tiffany grabbed one of his hands, trying to ease his tension. "I know it sounds crazy, and it may be too much to take in at once, but we've lost more than you know, Shadow. Our entire family is nearly gone and everything you see in front of you and around this area was rebuilt by Erica's hands. This is all we have left. These islands belong to us. It's been home ever since we lost all of you guys."

Shadow rubbed both hands across his face to ensure that he was hearing them both correctly. "Are you saying this because of what you've heard, or do you know this for sure? Did you see Ghost get buried inside of a casket?" he asked with a hurt expression.

Silence fell over them all, but Erica refused to lie. "No, but his father received word that he was gone. That was the last time we've ever heard from him."

"Just like when I went to New York, right?" Shadow asked, giving the indication that they may have been wrong.

Just as she was about to answer, Michael appeared in the doorway. He paused when he spotted his son's right hand man. His mind started to race, not knowing whether he should kill him at that exact moment. Their eyes locked for a slight second, and what was understood didn't need to be explained. His presence wasn't welcome and the vibe was more than mutual.

"I see you've decided to finally make your way back around the family. Unfortunately, my son isn't here, and we are trying to be cautious about who is allowed near my granddaughters. I don't mean any harm, but it's kind of awkward that you disappeared right after the demise of my son. You wouldn't know anything about that, would you?" Michael questioned with inquisitiveness.

Moving past Erica and Tiffany to stand face to face with the man who called himself a father, Shadow looked him square in the eyes. "No, unfortunately I don't, but I'm going to find out, and when I do, whoever is behind it will be soaking at the bottom of Guantanamo Bay. That's a promise. Sir," he spoke with emphasis before turning back to the two women he considered to be his close siblings. "I'll be back, but I need you girls to stay open minded to what's going on," he said just above a whisper for only them to hear.

Erica grabbed his forearm forcefully before he could keep walking. "You're not going anywhere!" Her slanted eyebrows told him that she was beyond serious, and the same expression was written all over Tiffany's face as well.

Shadow gently removed her hand and held it between his own. "Erica, relax, I'm coming back. I just need to find my brother because I know he's out there. You gotta trust me."

"Every time someone say that they're coming back, they end up dead," Tiffany added with sadness lacing her tone.

Shadow looked back and forth between them both before pulling them in for a hug. "I love you both, and I promise that i'm coming back, and I won't be alone," he guaranteed with a reassuring expression.

"You better," Erica warned before snapping her fingers towards one of her henchmen. "These are my men. They'll make sure you get to the airport and assist you along the way. Please don't let us down," she pleaded before grabbing Tiffany's hand and heading back inside.

"I won't," Shadow mumbled to himself before catching one last eye contact with Michael. The treacherous spirit inside of him could be felt emanating from his brown skin, and it was a feeling that could never be misinterpreted. He was a snake in plain form, and was surely gonna be the reason behind anything that occurred along the journey of Shadow's mission.

As Shadow stepped off the porch to leave the property, one of the large Yukon truck doors opened, giving him access to step inside. Two long dread head Jamaicans awaited inside. Trusting the word of his sister's authority, he climbed inside.

"Were ya wan go bad man?" the driver asked with a thick accent.

"The airport," Shadow replied before sitting back in his seat.

The nightmare of losing his friends and close associate was like the murder mystery from a James Patterson sequel. So much confusion had left a disastrous fate for them all, and now the bloodbath was resurfacing. Shadow knew that finding Ghost was gonna be a crippling mission due to all the targets aiming for his head, but one thing he knew for sure was that his brother would never let a casket be his resting grounds. It was a promise they made since the action started when the originals were holding the circle down with an iron fist. His mind moved too quickly for even the slickest, and nothing would reign supreme over the man who promised to dominate for the Grey family until all competition was demolished. Ghost was more than alive. He was slithering around with a mind of vengeance for one thing: to enforce the payback on everyone who crossed out the family of savages. The only thing Shadow had to do was prove that the dead man was far from resting, a task no one but himself could accomplish. He had to bring his partner in crime back to throne, or all they'd worked for was about to be snatched by the palms of a dirty Ramirez who claimed to be his father.

Chapter 4
Hartsfield Jackson Airport
Atlanta, GA

After running around the corners and back streets of Atlanta for a week, the conclusive info Torey had been looking for was finally spoken on. He had discovered the whereabouts of the man who played games with a ticking bomb's life. It wasn't pleasant knowing that his mission was leading him to another location, but for the life he wanted so badly, he was willing to travel across the world in order to see the fear run through his pupils like a trail of unforgettable tears. He could smell Ghost's life fading away with every step he made towards him.

Stepping foot inside of the large transportation ports, Torey inhaled the smell of victory approaching. His fingers were itching to see all the ones he could kill because of his uncle's stupid and outrageous decisions. The feeling was so good that he literally chuckled, anticipating the moment. His eyes slowly moved to the right and caught sight of Shadow's face. They were walking no further than twenty feet away from each other, but the expression that crossed his face once their eyes locked caused a small ounce of paranoia to crawl into Torey's mind. The eye lock lasted until they moved past each other, nearly brushing shoulders. Even though Torey kept his head forward, he could feel the creepy aura coming from the white man who had just mugged him up and down. Making a quick jolt for the bathroom hall, Torey placed his back against the wall. Just as he suspected, Shadow was walking backwards out the exit doors. Could have been a Fed. Maybe even a spy. Torey sure wasn't taking the chances on finding out. He was too close.

After watching the informant-looking motherfucker head out of the airport, Torey quickly made his way towards booking, looking up at the large boarding screen that read Virgin Islands. He smirked and headed swiftly up through the line. The first booking attendant he sighted, he dazzled his way up to the front. A few tourists poked their heads out of line with a glare of hatred. The boy dork at the lead looked too easy just to be standing in the number one service spot. A hundred niggas lined up, and all of them were waiting for the same response. Unfortunately, a few would always be snatched out of the bundle, and a slight amount would move with the intentions to kill another one. It only took one slip, so making it count this time was all Torey needed.

Pushing the geek from the small window, Torey cleared his throat. "Excuse me, Az-izzz," he sounded out while squinting at the name tag of the Arabian man that stood behind the window.

"It's Aziz, bro, that's it. Are you arriving in or leaving Atlanta?" he asked dryly.

"Leaving. I'm heading for the Islands to do my mixtape tour. Devils with no motive," Torey lied. "I expect to catch ya moms or sister there if possible. All the cool people will be present, so don't miss out," he boasted before throwing his ID and ticket into the flap.

"Sure. No thanks." The Arabian man's smile fell quickly to a frown as if "who gives a fuck" was written on the bottom of his shirt. Typing a few things into his computer, he sniffled loudly. "It says you arrived in Atlanta a week ago. Now you're off to the Rasta islands for an escape. I guess the scam life isn't up here with these fucking serial killers in Atlanta. They will shoot you for it. But that's not the point. How long will you be staying down there?"

"Damn, Aziz, y'all gotta know all that?" Torey spat, slapping the glass with an open hand.

"Well, Coronavirus says that's mandatory. So sorry to inform you."

"Well, in that case, I'll be staying forever." Torey smiled with a devilish grin.

Aziz gave him a strange look before stamping his document to leave. "Make sure to stay away from all dirty water, and wear your mask at all times."

"Yeah, yeah, fuck you, Kumar," he mumbled before grabbing the ticket and heading off to catch his flight.

The waiting line to board the plane for Jamaica wasn't that long. After he crossed the second rope, where an attendant stood, he pondered on the motherfuckers that would surely be willing to pay for their lives to be spared once he arrived to take back all the priceless things that were snatched away from him as a child. Those were mutual aches that he craved for Ghost to feel. It couldn't be dismissed unless it was personal and up close. That exact moment when he would be allowed to smell Ghost's last breath creeping up from his windpipe's floor…that was all the torn soul child wanted for his birthday. He grinned as he boarded the plane.

* * *

Stepping out into the fresh Atlanta air, Shadow looked around at the huge city. It wasn't the heart of the nasty stomping ground, but it sure wasn't far from it. After fifteen years of reckoning with the Pits of the Georgia home, he was finally back to slide through for another round. He knew that feeling invincible was more than superstitious. It was being too cocky, too arrogant to face that everyone in the world bleeds the exact same. That small dose of reality gave him enough courage to take on the entire city to find out if his fraternal twin was still kicking, and moving.

The first thing his eyes beamed in on was the rental car service that sat directly across the street. It wouldn't take long to get in a low-key vehicle and maneuver around the north side, College park, and Riverdale area where it was safe until nightfall. Once the sun was lightly snoozing, Shadow was gonna make his way over to the kitchen of Atlanta: the Westside.

* * *

Virgin Islands
The Grey mansion
9:43 p.m.

The small of sautéed shrimp and steak could be smelt creeping through the thick walls of Erica's home. It was another Monday night, and the chef was on point with the menu. There were also baked potatoes with all the fixings and a full bottle of Moet.

After stepping out of her hot shower, Erica tossed a champagne gold slip over her immaculate body. Her perky breasts were still a perfect C-cup, and not one man had come close to even seeing the color of her mocha brown nipples. Her heart molded into concrete within weeks of the news of Ghost's death, and the only person who was able to share her bed and gentle touches was Tiffany. A piece of her died years when Ghost made a departure from the family. The thought of Shadow popping up on her porch early this morning had her mind racing for inconclusive answers that she didn't have at the time. It wasn't a miracle, but it damn sho' wasn't for no reason.

The silky dress moved gently with her backside as she sashayed back and forth around the bedroom floor. Tiffany coming through the door caused her to freeze for a slight second. Her green eyes were the new trap that could get her into some deep steamy trouble within seconds, not to mention her stripper body had become more intoxicating to Erica as the times of not having a man straightening their backbone started to pass. She was her quick getaway when too much was exhausting her.

Erica wasted no time closing the distance and kissing her red lips gently. Their embrace was passionate as if it was the only form of love the two needed. Her caramel lip gloss was forcing her lips to protrude out in a pouty motion. Her skin was glowing from heading out in town to run errands, and all she could do was purr when Erica pecked them gently.

"How are you, love?"

"Nah, don't kiss me down, and ask how I'm doing. Why you all in the room like this, Erica?" She grabbed a hold of her thin dress and rubbed it with two thumbs. "And you dressing like we 'bout to fuck. Do you even have on panties?" Tiffany tried to lift her dress.

Erica grabbed both of her wrists. "I'm nervous, okay? If Shadow just popped out of nowhere saying that Ghost isn't dead, who's to say that he's not right?" Her eyes pleaded for a miracle. She had to know the truth. After searching the United States up and down for her King, she met enemies that eliminated her teams on sight. The word was eventually out. The price for Ghost's head was fifteen million for whoever could get him alive. The message was personally given by none other than Eva Ramirez herself. She was even bragging on the little demonic bastard Frost. Apparently her schizophrenic father didn't place enough bullets into her mother's head before he dropped his potent seed into her womb. Now, after ten long years of depression, more violence was approaching their residence quicker than a small wave cruising up on their beach backyard.

"Baby, you said that wasn't gonna be a thought. We've gotten our hopes up for this millions of times, and I don't want you to get upset like the last few times. We don't know where Shadow has been, but what more searching can he do that we haven't? I'm tired of seeing you hurt." She folded her arms across her juicy breasts.

Her Gray Valentino fitted shirt was cut with the rock girl slits just a tad over her breasts. Her matching blue jeans were glued on her thick thighs, and her red boots only made her open toes even sexier. She was gorgeous when she was mad, but it felt good that Erica had one person who could comfort her in the world. Their bond was deeper than the ancient music of Beethoven himself. It was a love she promised to never release on the strength of the rock who held them down so long. Wondering "what if" was her only failure.

"You looking good just to be going shopping and running errands with ya big booty ass. You got ya li'l duck-off boyfriend in that shopping plaza? If I catch him, I'll blow his brains through his esophagus." She grinned wickedly.

"I've never cheated on you, so hush that, and don't try to change the subject. If he's meant to come back, he will, but you can't build this energy up again and put all your faith in Shadow. He was just lost for ten years, Erica. He's been gone now for over twelve hours, and how do we know he coming back? It hurt me just to see his face. I can see he was confused, but he has confidence." Tiffany got close to her. "We gotta hope for the best and keep running the land, Queen. If we stumble, we lose."

Erica looked at herself in the distant mirror and snickered with a nod. "You're right. Maybe I do give good hope that one day he will be here. I've been losing it all since we started, and that's all I've asked for: my family." A light tear formed at her eyelid.

Tiffany wiped it and kissed her cheeks double times. "I love you. The kids need you, and these people down here in the tropics need you. Let's stand strong and see what else might come through. It only builds the momentum, because I would have a fucking heart attack." She giggled, thinking about Ghost's handsome face.

Erica threw on a fake cheese for her companion. After a decade of lock-in, that bolt still remained attached like it was closed by Iron Man himself. "I promise that we can go out tonight and have a blast. Guess why?" Erica asked with a secretive face.

"Why?"

"Because Reeses is in the car with Laylah and Stone. They're on their way from the airport. We're going for her bleed in and see the big girl you missed so much take a position at this family table. Ghost would love to see her brought in, especially after her arrival. Call all Jamaican clientele and let them know we're coming in for the bleed in. Have the funds right so they can be shipped immediately, love."

"That's the Erica I know." Tiffany smiled before twirling on her heels.

Before she could leave the room, Michael stepped in wearing a full black tux. His smooth black Gucci dress shoes were crispy, and his soft Puerto Rican hair laid gently down to his shoulders. His menacing face always made him seem as if something else was about to pop out of his mouth.

"Dinner is ready, girls. I thought we could share something to eat before you all head out tonight."

Tiffany sniffled lightly and brushed past him.

Erica hated his presence, but dealt with him on the strength of Ghost. Most of the time it seemed like he wanted to be the husband and ruler of the home instead of the son who had bled, murdered, and provided before he could even become a part of them. "Thanks. I'll be there in a minute." Erica ignored his invite and continued to stare out of the large window.

Sensing her unsettled body heat, he stepped deeper into the room. "Look, I know earlier that dude Shadow just popped up out of nowhere, making you believe those absurd words of his. If you remain focused, all will be well, and just like everyone else who claims that my son is alive, he will end up missing. He was a bad man when it came down to the way he moved. Love, for some, is different. It allows us to feel the way we want, instead of the way we should. You only know you love something when you let it go. I'll make sure the guards are prepared to get you all to Jamaica," he offered before turning to leave.

Once he stepped into the hall, he pulled out his cell phone and dialed the first number in his log. The call was picked up immediately.

"Yeah?"

"We need to find him and kill whatever problem he's trying to stir back up. I want Chance to remain dead. And make sure the poor guy at least gets a good funeral," Michael ordered, looking at his platinum Rolex watch.

"Consider it done. Once he's located, it's finished," the caller addressed before hanging up.

Michael straightened his shirt before he walked into the kitchen. Shit was lovely. Neither Erica nor Tiffany knew that after a while, certain orders were going to start being mandatorily enforced, if need be. His vision for building the perfect family was 20/20, and it was finally approaching the finish line. All he needed to do was keep closed doors sealed and keep old memories buried - at least until he found everyone connected to slice the Ramirez and Grey family into one. It was a family that he held control over, one that blood couldn't even think to go against.

Chris Green

Chapter 5
9th Ward, Delmar Lane, Allen Temple Apartments
Atlanta, GA

The late night was crawling deep up the night sky, and human zombies moved around on their destined missions. Some wanted to rob, maybe even sell a li'l pussy. It was a hellish path of never-ending backstabbing.

Shadow found himself lurking on a back trail to find any answers about his ace. The bond and word of family meant more than just life. It meant a promise he guaranteed they would keep forever, and that's what it was.

After pulling his car to the outside entrance, he shut off the engine and checked the Glocks that rested in his lap, sliding them onto his waist. As he got out of the car, a small crowd of thugs moved deeper inside the complex. It might have seemed weird that a white guy was out in a thugged-out neighborhood looking for a black guy who all of Atlanta was surely beefing with. But he knew that some answers were definitely about to come once he was sighted. By the time he strolled through the small field of grass to cross into the next building, a crew of Billy Blood gang members were posted in front of two vehicles. Half of them were already strapped with pistols in hand, and the foreign machine guns a few of them were clutching were bound to eat whatever flesh you came to offer for their feast.

"They people out chea whoa! Tighten up!" a voice yelled through the small rooftop breezeways when Shadow crossed the yellow bumper line.

The first Sox apartment doors opened with armed men in every doorway.

"Why you out here, dawg? You must ain't read our message?" Hotrod stood up off his car with a nasty gaze. His .32

extended clip was showing, and from the money knots cluttering his tight pockets, he had to be the leader. He was the exact motherfucker who Shadow needed.

Ignoring all the men aiming their guns recklessly, Shadow took a few steps forward. "I don't mean to intrude, bro."

"I'm not ya bro, cracker, and if you a cop, you better beat it before these folks kill you."

"Look, big homie, or whatever I need to say. I have a few grand for a little info on my friend. I'm not a fuckin' cop." Shadow snatched up his shirt, exposing the handle of his pistol after a few men raised a few of their weapons closer to his head. "I'm solid just like anyone of y'all. All I need to know is if anybody has seen or heard from him around this way. I'm an old friend, and I really need to find him." He pulled two grand out in crispy hundreds and held them out to Hotrod.

Their gazes locked for a minute too long. All the hooded men and sectioned-off groups in the little apartment buildings could have easily killed him upon entering, so obviously somebody had some say. A few citizens stared out of their windows, and more armed hoodlums stood in the background, as if they were standing guard in case the authorities got alerted.

Hot Rod grinned at the money before grabbing it. None of the men reached for Shadow's gun, and he was surprised that the tension ceased immediately when he agreed to what was said. "You saying you looking for somebody. It ain't no white people live out here, fool. This the Mob spot. Who the fuck you supposed to be on this death quest for, man?" Hot Rod cuffed the check in his front pocket.

Shadow huffed. "His name is Ghost. I know this is an area he used to move around, and I needed to know if anybody heard from him or seen his presence."

"Who?" Hot Rod wiggled a finger in his ear, quickly leaning forward.

"Ghost."

"That name ain't getting mentioned around here unless a nigga 'bout to lose his cap. Don't speak on him, and he leaves us be. You chasing a nigga that none of us can even get a clear picture of. That's a search you gotta discover on ya own, my fella, but it was good doing business with you." He waved him off before turning back around to his female company.

"Hey, one last thing?" Shadow pulled out another thousand. "What side does he usually make his motions in?"

Hot Rod walked smoothly over to him and slid the cash from between his fingers. "All you have to do is follow the news. He has a list, so be careful, and try not to make it if you not who you say you are. Try Niggerville. Down bottom towards the West End. Keep that noise on the low," he explained before turning his back.

Shadow nodded, accepting the small piece of knowledge from the young gangster. No one was willing to speak for free, and you had to pay in order to get a sprinkle of truth, which was nothing compared to what was at stake. He was hearing clearly from another person that people only heard his name when motherfuckers started winding up dead. That sounded exactly like his dear brother. But now it was time to search and find out what was left to play with. Either he was coming back to the islands with Ghost, or he was going back to ensure that Michael was stopped with the sneaky plot he was devising right under Erica's nose.

Getting back to his car, he blew out a breath of relief and started his engine. He lit up the fresh blunt in his ashtray box. He turned up the volume of his stereo, allowing Meek Mill's song "Ambition" to beat through his speakers. It was more of

Ghost's music choice, but in order to think brilliantly like him, you had to take the steps to become him.

Doing a full doughnut, Shadow mashed the gas, heading in the opposite direction. Getting caught slipping again was a no-no, and he refused to leave without digging into every hater or supporter when it came down to his best friend. If the murder game had to be placed back down, then the streets of Atlanta could welcome their demon back home. In order to find the killer, you had to be the killer.

Chapter 6
Eva's penthouse suite, Manhattan, New York
2:14 a.m.

She opened her eyes from the loud yelling in the living area. Frost sat up in her bed and reached for her pistol on the nightstand. Once she realized it was Eva having a heated phone conversation, she stood up from the bed and sighed with anger. She was sporting a Tommy Hilfiger sports bra and pair of matching pajama shorts that a mama would have probably strangled their baby for wearing back to school in the old days. Her flawless skin was redder than a tan specialist's. She was perfectly proportioned from her head to feet. The curly honey blonde hair was another fatal attraction given to her from Coco. In two days, she was turning eighteen, and her only wish was to reap the soul of her father and make him beg for his pitiful mistakes. Death was all she could dream of. It was the only thing that could make her cum with satisfaction, knowing that someone who disgraced her family's worth was handled accordingly.

She made it to the living room with Eva. Eva was at the table with two empty bottles of V.S.O.P. Her wine glass was still half full as she cursed silently to herself. Her right hand rubbed her temple in order to gain a second of peace from the lousy failures surrounding her. She had spent years playing the game, jumping from state to state - California, Nevada, Delaware, Atlanta - all to find one man: the nephew who caused her entire life as she knew it to be disintegrated horribly after he killed her father Jesus in his own home. She later found out that her three boys received his disturbing visit, and it was a battle that none of them were able to rise up against, no matter how hard Jesus bred them to be heartless.

"Are you okay? I heard you talking," Frost asked before setting her gun on the table.

Eva broke out of her slump and smiled. "I am now. You asked me what I had for your birthday, and I think I finally want to tell you." She chuckled evilly and it was like a baritone dude needed to be humming behind her or some shit.

"What did you get? If it's another Maserati, I'm taking it back to the dealership myself," she replied while grabbing a bottle of water from the fridge.

"No, no cars, baby girl." Eva leaned up before crossing her leg swiftly over one another. "I think you need to brighten your special day. I found your father's little pet, and after all this time, our people found him scavenging around the city looking for your lovely dad. This really may be your chance to see if the dead piece of shit really is still flopping around like a bruised fish without water."

"Don't play with me, Eva. I don't need your trickery right about now. So the sad-ass white man has come out from hiding? If anybody can find the reckless piece of shit they call my father, it will damn sure be him." Frost jumped up with excitement.

"Calm down. We have eyes on him, and if we receive the right call, I'll let you get to his destination and allow you to cut him from the gut up to his neck. Everybody wants to sink their teeth into the fifteen million that me and Pauly placed on his peanut head."

"We could've found this bozo years ago and taken care of all my pathetic sisters at the same time. I'm tired of traveling to nowhere, and I don't see the purpose in chasing these bitches and slimeball sperm donor. I want him alive, and his friend will suffice if no one can track down this retard. I'll pay extra." She leaned forward on the table with a look of objection. "What's the catch?"

"There is none, darling. We've searched until we've found an answer. Now all he has to do is lead us to the one we need. Then the curtains shall close for the Grey family. This is the moment we waited for. Not only will you have your revenge, but you can have fun at the same time. Now it's all just the matter of a phone call. "Eva plotted sipping a swallow of her fresh alcohol.

Frost stood up, and grabbed her gun. Placing it into the small of her back. She licked out her tongue. I'm gonna grab a shower for good luck, and pray that these sorry ass guards could make this happen for a change. I'm tired of spending money to keep me busy, Auntie. You make me think you and my mom have gotten soft on me." She laughed before walking off.

No one wanted to see the child when she was furious. A temper like hers would force a mack daddy-ass pimp to pull the trigger on his damn self. She was a bundle of sexiness and wicked explosion mixed together. Her sweet face would make you feel that no harm was done. She was a girl that you could easily allow to sleep on your couch overnight because of her breaking down, the same brat you would never expect to be filthy rich. She was a trained combat fighter in two countries, and the best woman that ever picked up a pistol within the Ramirez family. She was the baby, but trained to perfection for moments like the present one.

Making her way through the gigantic suite, she headed back down the hallway and slid over to her personal bathroom. Her beautiful face was posted in the mirror with a look as if the world was hers. She knew that if she wanted domination over all the Grey family, everyone down to her two big sisters had to be eliminated. That was the way she was taught, and the last war was only paused, but never dead.

She dug her nails deeply into her arm skin. The pleasure was gonna be so nice.

* * *

Little Five Points
Downtown Atlanta
Two days later

Shadow pulled his black RAM truck into the Garnett train station's parking lot. He placed the whip in park and cut the music completely off. It had been two days now since he arrived in Altman and all the same shit was coming out of everyone's mouth. Ghost was never to be mentioned or else shit was going to get ugly for the one speaking. He was now the most closed mouth nigga in the district. No one clarified that he was pushing daisies, and he could tell that the fear his partner instilled was deeply engraved into the grounds of every neighborhood. The only thing he knew for sure was that Reeses's name was bumping through the blocks harder than Lil Wayne's album. News about her being incarcerated a few months back was going around fast, and the men who she left out in charge of the street operation were forcing nothing but the money mission and getting out of there. Niggas wasn't slipping about that paper route, and a plentiful amount of cash was a great reason to leave a bitch stuck like some glue on a concrete brick. Unfortunately, Jimmie's daughter could give him no help if she was behind the wall, and her street crew could only go so far for the white cop-looking guy who came in the hood to get some reliable answers.

After driving around from the west to the south, Shadow maneuvered out to the north side and still had no luck. Either there was a scary-ass mystery tale about Ghost that had motherfuckers shook and scared to talk, or he was around laying down his body count in order to measure out how he was gonna move on with his next objective.

The sun was just lowering below the horizon, and the Hotlanta heat was starting to simmer down into a cool laidback breeze. The evening junkies were crawling out of the nearest corner stores, and the precinct was starting to make their daily roll-in with a quota of a hundred crooks to catch a day. That spot alone forced Shadow a stomach to turn, and seeing a cop was the last thing he wanted.

Placing his car in drive, he headed out of the gated lot and towards the mall. The sight of Magic City strip club forced him to smile. The days where he and Ghost used to slide in the spot to get a little moment of relaxation always ended with a freak bitch reliving a story that she cherished him years before they really even knew each other. It was a spot where all laughs were non-ending. It was even crazier that it was the only spot where the smiles never ended until it was time to leave.

Gazing at the woman on the club's banner, he shrugged his shoulders and pulled inside. It was nearly going on 8:36, and his foot had been pressing the pedal to search and find what he was looking for. A break was never guaranteed, and playing with fire was like caring for a small infant when it came down to the true beast that was inside of him. He didn't need that side to come back, but it would if necessary. He prayed that his mind showed darker but better visions than the usual ones he'd been receiving.

Climbing out of the large Ram truck, he sparked a cigarette and tossed on his black leather jacket. His pistol was now tucked into his armpit holster, and it wasn't going to be removed willingly or forcefully. The early time limit could gain him an easy entrance to the booty club, but as always, there was one fake big chain-ass nigga holding post out front. You could tell he wasn't official security from the dirty-ass Jordan's he had tied on his feet extra tight. His camo cargos were fading like a dry erase marker on plastic. The only thing he had half way decent was his five dollar fake twenty thousand dollar piece that was sparkling every time the light touched it.

His face flipped to killer as soon as Shadow started to step up the small few stairs that led to the entrance. "Uhhh, you sure Magic is what you trying to find, huckleberry? They have a Hooters bar right down the street." He laughed before slapping hands with the hoe-ass nigga posting up with him.

"Nah. This is the spot. It feels good hitting a big ole black ass. Pussy fat like a Russian sheep. I'm paying for bitches like this while you're catching the nearest dope heads from Backpage. I can't wait to get in here and spend this li'l money." Shadow smiled, holding out his fist with a rookie expression.

Leaving his shit dangling, the poor time security made him post against the wall for a pat down. After checking his jacket, he rubbed down both his pants legs and paused. Reaching under his arm, he felt the handle of his gun, and took a few steps back.

"Ay, man. You sure getting some ass is the only thing you came here tonight for?" the older dude asked cautiously.

"I'm positive. Just a good time. The protection is like my skin, folk. Here's a little somethin' to take your chick out tomorrow," he said before handing him two hundred dollar bills and walking inside.

The loud music could be heard quaking through the glass door before he fully entered the building. As always, ass was going bonkers on the Monday special night. Bottles of champagne and liquor were in the air, which was flooded with the sparkles of expensive watches and rings. Dollar bills filled the floor in front of him, and it was finally a spot that made him feel like home was kind of missed after all. Megan Thee Stallion's song "Savage" was whamming through the woofers, and bitches was laying their entire skeleton out, trying to throw their damn hips for a buck.

Shadow headed for the bar first and grabbed his usual. "A Heineken, and a shitload of Hennessey, no ice.," he requested before sliding a fifty dollar bill across the counter.

The lights were fading on and off as the club put on for a new chick's performance. Thick clouds of smoke were flooding that area so seeing clearly was not about to happen unless you had ya face on a bitch's pelvic bone.

"Here you go, sir," the waiter said before setting down his order.

Just at that moment, his phone rang before he could even take a sip. He pulled it out and slid the answer bar across. "Yeah?

"Shadow, have you heard anything yet? It's been two days, and I wanted to make sure you were okay," Erica lied, wanting to know exactly what he had discovered.

"Yeah, sistas been a drag session, but…" He paused when his eyes landed on a dude with his back turned in the corner with a cute woman. His posture was too familiar, and from the look of his Boosie fade, he could sense that the man's identity had to be one that he could easily remember. "Erica, I'm gonna call you right back, okay?" he said slowly into the line.

"What happened? Did you find anything?"

He couldn't even reply, and all his hands could do was slide his cell back up. He was trying to lean in for a better visual on the man who caught his attention, but he didn't want to look like a fucking groupie brushing up on a nigga that was unknown. The only thing that forced a stumble in Shadow's heart was the smile the man wore when he turned his head to the side. Without hesitation he stood to his feet and headed over for the dark section. The traits of a brother never changed, and he could probably tell you the smallest things about his homie before his own women could. It was the reason their connection shined over the average respect and love.

The closer he got, the more he could see the man's image forming together. Before the woman could finish her last dance, he was standing behind them both with a look of violence wrapped on his expression.

"Uh, do you owe this guy some money, or is he your parole officer?" the woman whispered into his ear before standing up to leave.

Not once did he turn to look behind him. He could feel the aura floating off his surprise guest's body heat, but panicking was never gonna be a part of the mission. Taking a sip of his Hennessey out of the bottle, he exhaled.

"So to whom do I owe this attempt to? You're not gonna make it out this club thinking about harming me in any kind of way, sucker, that's a promise. Now will I turn around and kill you in two point four seconds is the motherfucking question you need to be asking yourself." Ghost turned up his bottle one last time before preparing to make his move.

"First of all, I send my goddamn self to kill anybody, and I'm damn sure not gonna get hurt by these bogus-ass bodyguards you have fake securing the premises. I could've just killed them all on my way in. The only reason I approached is because you look like an old friend of mine. I guess I was wrong." Shadow could tell by the reaction of the fool he was talking to that nothing was close about them at all, until Ghost turned around in his chair. "Now the second rule is to always make sure you check who you dealing with in case they play the role. Third, we don't give a damn how nice you are or how cooperative."

"Yo' ass had to go," they said in unison before Shadow jumped into his dawg's arms.

"I should beat you with a monkey wrench, you fucking bastard! Can you tell me how in the fuck I lost my best friend for the past ten years?" Shadow was looking at him with a huge grin, waiting for an answer, but instead, he got a quieter Ghost. He even took a seat before looking back up into his rich hand man's face.

"Shit has changed, Shadow. Beef isn't the same no more. I found out after I left my home to end a war that I created one under my own roof, and I didn't pay attention. I placed the girls in jeopardy." He lowered his head, ashamed for the losses he suffered along the way.

Shadow pulled up a chair directly in front of him. They sat a few feet away from each other and couldn't help but to laugh. It had been so long since they were last in each other's presence. Now the thoughts that had been eating at him for so long could finally be answered.

"How did you find me?" Ghost asked, tossing back another shot. The long scar running down the side of his face kept Shadow's eyes looking at his brother with a look of hurt.

"Who did that to you? Give me a small break down of what is going on, bro, 'cause right now, I'm fucking lost."

"Michael pulled a slimeball move on me and tried to have his li'l personal security do me in if I didn't choose to stay away. My home, the shit I worked years to build… It was just taken by a nigga that left me for twenty-two years. Now he comes back and plots the unthinkable. The hits that's been called since back then in New York was coming from Michael. It was the reason they knew our whereabouts, the reason Dio, Mark, and Even Tim lost their lives. He wasn't en route to mending a father and son relationship with us. He was coming to take back what he wanted to have."

Ghost wasn't involved with that picture at all. After escaping Michael's associate, he eventually had a chance to think back about his movements and the way Michael would sit back and observe as he operated. He offered opinions and a helping hand every now and then, but as long as the show was going, he was always present and calm for whatever occurred. He was already cautious of the danger Ghost could cause, so getting rid of him the easy way was like tricking a dog with a fake bone. Throw it out there, and wait for a bite.

"I let him play me out of the comfort of my own home. My girls down there without me, and I know he means to so-called murder me if I step foot back through the Islands airport. Since I know his résumé of making that type of shit happen, I've decided to smash on all the outsiders until the moment is right for me to creep back to the rock."

"Folk, the time is now. Those girls are a wreck without you, bro. It's been ten long years, and shit isn't the same in these people's hearts, Ghost. Fuck Michael. We either go and take back what's yours and get rid of him, or we can war with them all just like we used to. The choice is really yours. I made a promise to return back alive to Erica and Tiffany. That also included you if I had a chance to lay my own eyes on you. I know it's been a while, dawg, and shit could seem crazy in your head right now. But trust me, your children and women need you. A bigger crash is coming for them, and if you're not there, death is bound to take them all out. From the looks of it, they held your name together well, but I don't know how long they can go through never having closure. We need to go." Shadow crossed his fingers and leaned in closer to his friend.

Ghost rubbed a hand across his chin forcefully. It was a deadly game to place the girls at risk knowing how dangerous his dad could get. A long journey away from home was made, but it hadn't been consecutive. A few stops were made, and a couple of whispers were always left, but missing his Queens, and Princesses was becoming difficult. That chain of adhering to his first mind was out the window, and now that his personnel was sitting down back in front of him after a major split, Shadow's advice was genuine. It would never change.

"Fuck it, I guess I'll be coming home." Ghost smirked with a grin of hatred. "You might wanna leave out of here separate though."

"What the hell do you mean? Shit has been separated long enough. We leaving out that damn door together."

"Listen, bro, it's been a few long years, and this beef is bigger than a cow's ass on Depo birth control shots. I literally have to gun at some shit every day, and from the looks of it, I'm about to be involved with incident number three within a few minutes," Ghost added before taking a small swig of the sweet liquor.

The dude who was walking over to them damn sure didn't come in with them, so he obviously had other plans. A small Mac 90 was cuffed in his hands, and he was calmer than calm when he arrived over to them and raised his gun. "Y'all idiots be smart, and let's give Eva what she wants. If you obey, I won't kill you in front of these people," he threatened with a weak-ass tone.

"Hey, I believe you, but you gotta worry about all these people, man. Someone is obviously gonna try to be a hero." Ghost flashed him a scary look.

"Fuck that. Get up——" was all he got out before Shadow smashed the barrel of his gun into the man's Adam's apple.

Ghost followed up and two-pieced him viciously, sending his unconscious body to the ground.

"It's okay, everyone. We're police officers!" Shadow yelled to everybody while holding up a fake badge. The main attention was placed on the entrance and getting the hell out of harm's way before it could sniff them out.

The club attendants looked on as the fellas made their way out of the two glass double doors. The sixteen men that stood in the parking lot were obviously waiting for a sticky situation to unfold, and now the action was closer than his jugular vein.

"Gentlemen, I think we have business to attend to." One of the head men dressed in black moved towards them with an assault rifle dangling in his hands.

Before any question could be responded to or restated, Ghost, and Shadow did what they did best. Both of their guns were pulled from their bodies in a flash, and Ghost couldn't even aim correctly without letting off fifteen shots. Shadow followed suit, allowing his gun to quake directly beside his own.

Bloc! Bloc! Bloc! Bloc! Bloc! Bloc! Bloc!

Pak! Pak! Pak! Pak! Pak! Pak! Pak!

The bullets erupted, allowing them to dash around the club building for a quick run and escape on foot. Their feet could be heard crushing against the trash behind the strip joint while running for cover. A few of the parked cars that were posted in the front came flying towards the back, and there was no telling what they were trying to show and prove. Bending down, Ghost hit the driver's side of the windshield three times before dashing through the thin woods behind Shadow.

Boc! Boc! Boc!

One of his slugs found its destination through his nose cavity, killing him quicker than the blade of a fan doing a complete spin.

"How you let me get my crack backkk!" Ghost laughed wickedly while a few of the men tried to release a few bullets instead of following behind.

Pakkkk! Pak! Pak! Pak! Pak! Pak! One of the semis ripped away harshly forcing the grass shreds to scatter wildly. After shooting nearly a hundred bullets, they stopped just to see that they hadn't hit shit. The two targets weren't waiting behind the short path of bushes, and once again, the two devil twins of the playground were back united.

"How in the fuck did I let you get me into this?" Shadow asked as they ran at a medium pace up the backstreet.

"You said you love me, nigga! Well, love it the fuck up. It's time to go home." Ghost snickered, raising his reloaded gun.

"I'm not ready to dash and slash motherfuckers right now, but if we're not out of here by tomorrow, the entire town will know we're back, bro. It's not good to expose ourselves so quick with all that's going on, asshole!"

"Just one last thing, cream puff. One more person to see tonight, and by morning, we can fly high to the Bob Marley side," he assured him as they made it to his tinted-out Dodge Demon Sport.

The engine coming to life growled like a lion that hadn't eaten in the past week. Hitting the steering shift, Ghost swerved in a U-turn, heading back for expressway 1-75. The loud Taylor Swift song "Reputation" blasted through his vehicle, and of course his glove compartment was filled with rolled doobies. Sparking one, he laughed hysterically.

"What the fuck is funny, fucktard?" Shadow spat, looking into the head visor mirror. A few scratches were on his face, but overall, everything seemed to be okay.

"'Cause, fool, we're back at our usual, and I don't care about shit when I feel like that!" he cried out with a smile before pulling on his weed.

It didn't take long to reach the highway, and after twenty minutes of driving, Ghost had arrived at the Camp Creek area.

The plaza was beyond packed and you could see the variety of women moving around like it was a safe haven for all relationships. It was life, and everyone chose to live it how they pleased. Your choices were made consciously, and that was the reason mercy and compassion got such a tough time coming free from his spirit. The losses he took were irreplaceable, and nothing could change it for the better.

Turning down the loud pop star's music, Ghost swigged his hot soda from earlier and frowned. "Damn, that shit nasty. I think my little buddy should already be here too," he added, pulling into the Applebee's restaurant.

"Wait. What the fuck are you doing, going on a date? We need to grab your shit and be out." Shadow was gripping his pistol with a spooked trigger finger just in case an ounce of something looked out of place.

The last incident just involved too many investigating Expedition trucks, and about three dead. Four were wounded in the leg or arm. Minor condition was their last report after the radio spilled the beans on the expressway. The wind was gusting like a bitch, and it was damn sure the weather to run into a pack of foot officers driving down the street.

"Bro, this shit is pretty simple. You know who I'm going to see, and there's a few more on the list. I can't miss these appointments, Shadow. They've already been made." He gave him a smooth smirk. "Come in with me. Please, man." He pulled out a weird-ass old Kangol and a dirty fitted Cardinals hat.

"Fuck, man." Shadow grabbed the shabby-ass barber hat and covered his head and eyes. Ghost followed suit and pulled the red hat down over his face like he was straight from up top. They both checked their guns and got out at the same time, making their way inside.

Shadow cleared his throat. "So who exactly are you gonna kill in front of all these hungry-ass watching customers?"

"A stupid person," he whispered back before the waitress arrived to the front panel check in.

"Hi guys. How many will you be seating?"

"Just a table for me and my buddy." Ghost smiled.

"Okay, follow me."

They trailed the small little black girl through the aisle. She found them a small section that was empty.

Taking their seats, Ghost ordered a Sprite immediately. "With fresh squeezed lemons, please." He tapped the table.

She stood there dumbfounded for a second before eventually pushing off to do her job.

Looking behind a few seats, Ghost spotted Tweety waving lightly and motioned her to come over. Shadow huffed with sympathy when he saw her pathetic face. The only thing he wasn't filled in on was the part where she played in the family death scandal also. Apparently she was a walking camera following his moves, someone else Eva was using to handle dirty issues. Turns out that Tweety knew about the entire set-up. She knew that Coco was in hiding for the coma and had a child while in critical state. Ever since he first met Tweety at the club in California - the dance, the pussy – it was all trash. It was sad in her case that she didn't know what Ghost became aware of recently. The time for bouncing around the clubs was finally coming to an end. The sea creature was here for the confrontation.

"Hey Zaddy." She pranced over to their section as if it was the happiest day of her life, sliding in the booth side next to Ghost. He cringed when she kissed his face with joy. "Damn, boy you got war wounds and shit. This part of the reason I haven't seen you in forever?" she asked with a serious face. Her hair was nice in a French curl at the edges. Her red H&M

sweater matched her Gianni slacks, and a Frances Valentine bucket bag was pulled tightly over her arm. Her eyelashes were highlighted, and she gazed at him and Shadow for a minute before asking her question. "Ghost, how have you really been? This doesn't look like the old you. Your face wounds make you look like the whole devil. A handsome one, of course, but I mean, how have you tried to relax, and free yourself from things, ya know?" Tweety asked, feeling her time for a sweet loan was in need.

"Shit, I'm better than a nacho plate at Rice Street on store day. How you been living lately?" He stared up into her face with his soulless eyes.

"Umm, I'm actually a school teacher now."

"No! Seriously?" Ghost gasped sarcastically.

"Yeah, I teach elementary and second grade substitute when they need an extra fill in."

Ghost fumbled to catch his phone. It slid past Tweety's leg, and hit the floor. "Damn, can you get that for me, ma?" He pointed underneath the tablecloth and by the time she reached under it, he locked her quickly into a death grip chokehold. Her arm was tangled behind her, and all his body weight was leaning down on her as he tightened the grip around her neck.

Her feet forced Shadow to kick them down repeatedly until her little body frame gasped for heaven. She was so folded up into the seat that her body slid down under the table as if it was made to be her bed. Shadow looked around the restaurant and shit was still moving better than smooth. No one saw the black girl that sat at the table with a death date. It was an easy payback without having to give the long explanation why.

Placing a twenty dollar bill on the table, they both stood to their feet and abandoned the table without another question. Shadow looked back at Ghost once they hit the parking lot.

"Hey, I came to save your ass for what needs to be your priority, not include myself in personal fun along the way. Let's just find a better way to deal with people in the open. The bitch is under the table dead in Applebee's, dawg." Shadow got to the passenger door, and got in.

Ghost jumped in beside him with a calm attitude. "I know you haven't seen me in a while, and shit has changed drastically. But we gotta be careful saying that I'm stepping back on the Islands to stay. I'll handle the business with Michael one on one, but I don't wanna risk any of the girls getting hurt. I've sucked in one thing that old bastard said, and he's right. Every time I come around my ladies or my children, evil shit happens towards them. It kinda forced me to stay away even longer. How do I know it all ain't good down there or if my two daughters are healthy and rich with no flaws? Seems like shit was going better than good, and I'm not trying to murder the last piece of my blood I got. Especially the nigga who's the reason I'm here on this earth to have y'all in the first place."

"Ghost it's the other way around. If it wasn't for your mother, you wouldn't be here. The dads were just sex slaves and deadbeats. We had our faith 'cause they were the old man, but I realized one thing after a while, bro. We all have choices to go by, and if our relationships turn out shitty, it's obviously from one side of the field or the other. In this case, you didn't even have the ball enough in range to get a first down. Now I'm here to help my family, the promise we made when we were thirteen. They need us, bro," Shadow stated with caution.

Ghost listened with a quiet nod. It was clear that what he was saying was indeed the truth, but it didn't leave his mind. He couldn't place his baby girls in jeopardy while dealing with the mind of a psychopath. No one could understand it when you grew up in a regular home with normal responsibilities.

Things become different when you grow to work for a family business of drug dealers and killers for hire. There would never be a day of correct moving when you constantly stayed on the move for lots of money transactions and mutual agreements. He was burning inside to know what was coming next, but there was no other way. Ghost was beyond missing his daughters and two ride or dies through whatever. They were more than worth the fight, and if that meant he had to murder that last trace of his bloodline, then it was done.

"Look, we can go back tonight. Word around the Island is my dad calls shots without Erica even being around. He's basically sat up a defense to be able to protect himself if shit went left, or——"

"Try and take Erica, and the girls for his own personal slaves," Shadow finished off his remark. "I saw it in his eyes when I popped over to your house. He didn't want me there, and I can damn sure bet that if Erica wouldn't have shown me so much love and help, I would have probably been dead before I could make it off that Island. Trust me, dawg, Erica isn't the same gullible Fed. She's a full-fledged queenpin for the entire south. You are all she's missing. But we gotta move now."

"We do it my way. I can't just stroll through the front door asking my dad did he secretly plot to fuck my wives and gain power over my operation after his fuckboy bodyguard tried to murder me. I'm not trying to see him pull a slick one on some dangerous shit with them in the crib. I'll allow him to get comfortable and pull up close enough where he can smell what I ate this morning. I don't need no funny moves, or thoughts because I'm not hesitating," he warned, pushing the heavy duty motor towards his duck-off apartment.

"I'll be right there the entire time, and nothing will go wrong if we just do what needs to be done. I can guarantee it." Shadow gave him a look of confidence.

"I'll believe that once I cross that bridge. After we get to this spot, I'm grabbing all cash and important shit. We have a private flyer that can have us on the Virgin rock within six and a half hours. There's no turning back after this, and if I die, I'll do it fighting for what I loved." Ghost shrugged, preparing his mind for what was next.

It was time to take the high chair of his operation. The devil was back, and he wanted it all, even if it caused gallons more blood to be spilled for what was his. Nobody was taking shit. But actions were better proven when displayed instead of conversating. The game was starting, and only one could be prepared. Winners smiled, and losers wept. Dumb decisions make reckless beasts.

Chris Green

Chapter 7
Virgin Islands, the Grey Mansion

The huge-ass ceilings were growing by the second as Erica laid on the giant queen-sized French made mattress. After catching up on a powerful new venture that would send them higher with the dues and earnings, she called a family sit down. Profits were accumulating faster than last year's drive. The connections was flying in from upstate and all surrounding locations including Puerto Rico and Cuba. The price of twenty a kilo sounded steep to a broke hustler, and it was a light form of mercy from the talk of how potent her poison was. Not even the richest punk from the outskirts of Dominican Republican could offer more than a three hundred thousand dollar exchange, and Erica declined it all.

She was sharing a bath with Tiffany as their personal assistant held her feet out of the exquisite bathing bowl to paint a coating of stripes over her French toenail manicure. She took personal time with her girls and constantly stressed how important it was to look at all the outsiders as enemies. Nobody can show that love like family. She didn't give a floppy dick about the cash or business if it didn't truly possess ever essential peace. Guns did the killings, not the one who pulled the trigger. A begging bitch would do whatever when they were in need of something they were craving, whether it was for a reputation, rumor, or confirmation that the shit actually works if you pull the fucking trigger. Erica was sure to build her knowledge and embed the fact that no one will ever truly be one hundred percent official with you without bringing along something false. While niggas expected her structure to be feeble and profit less without Ghost, she began to show why her name was changed to Mrs. Grey. When dealing with customers, if a person showed any sign of treachery, she would have them executed directly in front of her. There was only a certain amount of meetings she was willing to take on within a week, and when disrespect started to build and people started to think a woman couldn't be more vicious than a snapping pit, she proved them wrong. If a customer was a dollar short on, Erica was executing him while the sun was shining bright. If a man or competition felt that their backgrounds didn't match the images they were making them out to be, personal visits were made within hours and you were immediately murdered. Seven so-called cocaine gods were placed on that scratch chart when a few millions started to come up missing from the spots where shit was placed. Money was flowing in, but out faster with all the slime-ass tricks she had become a victim too. It took a lot of growth, but the reformed Erica was respected for the great mind she carried. Nothing was able to break her down when it came to feeding and spoiling Ghost's two grownish, and experimental-ass daughters.

The doorbell rang loudly, forcing her to jump out of bed and into her flat slide-on Versace's. They were suede gray, matching the smoke grey jeans on her heart-shaped bottom. Her pistol was attached in her holster, and she could feel the sweat forming under her fitted Jill Stuart top. Her light makeup gave her the Miss America shine, and she was looking edible, as always. The adrenaline to answer the door forced her to make it through the long corridor until she reached the entrance of their home. Tiffany was making her way down the second floor flight of stairs, so they reached the designation at the exact time.

Erica looked up at Tiffany before taking a slow deep breath. Her head was spinning, and it was either the moment for another heartbreak, or a devastating blackout that usually ended with a dark cloud under the house roof. Tiffany stepped down behind her just as she reached for the knob, opening the entrance to their expensive residence. Her small smile formed when she noticed that it was Shadow, but no sight of anyone with him forced it to fall. Tiffany placed a kiss on her cheek before wrapping an arm around her hip.

With a low whisper, Tiffany said. "Be easy, and let's give him a chance to see what he found out, at least. If we drop our faith now, it'll never prosper for us. Maybe he's heard something different then what we've been fed for years."

Erica nodded, knowing that her logic made perfect sense. She fiddled with her fingers nervously as a few of her armed Jamaican shottas escorted him inches away from the doorway. Erica waved them off and leaned over to give her brother a warm hug of gratefulness before he explained anything. His dedication for trying was more than appreciated, but there were still opened doors that she truly wanted closure for.

"Come in. You don't have to stand out here like a stranger." She grabbed his forearm, walking him smoothly inside.

The paint color on the walls, down to the matching furniture, was able to settle his spirit. It was as if he was back at Ghost's mom's crib back in their wilder days. It smelt richer than rich, and he nearly grew exhausted walking from the entrance to the family resting area. Tiffany walked over to the flat screen hanging in the wall and turned it down. The feeling she had was already confirmed on the low just from the way Shadow was looking, but she didn't want to anger Erica any more by forcing pain back into the walls of her heart.

Shadow looked around the upscale home and took a seat on the couch behind him. Erica stood a few feet away from him anticipating for him to give any other sign that there was hope. Tiffany posted against the side of the gold mantel piece, shaking her head.

"I know that I've been gone a few days, and I promised to be back sooner, but it was a damn drag session. The bad news is that I haven't heard anything official about the death of him personally, but the fear Atlanta has over them tells me that somebody ain't playing fair when the sun drops. I couldn't find him, but I think there is still a chance," he lied hoping that she didn't have a mental breakdown on his ass.

"Wait." Erica held up a finger while folding her lips in anger. "You mean to tell me that no one in that entire city has any info on my man? After all the shit he gave and saved for their selfish asses? You can start back sending a few morning visits to see if that stirs some shit up, since no one has anything to speak about." Her voice seethed with a scowl.

Tiffany slowly shook her head, knowing that her emotions were about to take a trip out of the house, and she truly didn't want to sit around just to say she said so about not getting their hopes high. The thought alone had her ready to cry like a baby. He was a locked door in her head that she tried greatly to keep sealed enough to keep her rage and twisted thoughts caged away. There were times before where she never allowed any person regardless of rank or position go against their reputation and hard work for that number one spot. Those times seemed so strong and powerful. All that she understood couldn't be enforced the same without him. That alone drove Tiffany's heart into a deep space.

She spotted Michael walking down the stairs, adjusting the sleeves to a J.M Weinstein button down. Refusing to hear him add anything to fuel the fire, she peeled out, leaving the conversation where it began. She was gonna take a breather and find something constructive to attend to until the anger subsided. She picked up the laundry bucket in the hallway. She tuned in on Erica's voice, which was obviously getting louder to Shadow's response, before heading upstairs.

Michael folded his arms once he spotted Erica speaking with his son's little baby protector. His presence didn't mean shit but one thing: he was about to stick his nose in some business that didn't need his involvement. He continued to talk about the small details he discovered as Erica rocked her leg with a forceful shake. The annoyance on her face was all it took for him to butt in.

"Hey man, what the hell are you doing?" Michael questioned with a toxic stare. "Now you've come back here with foolishness that's only gonna reactivate old devastation that's better off remaining asleep, stressing her out with whatever lies you've tried to keep them away from. I don't know what your mission is, buddy, but I'm always around - watching, waiting, like an eagle's eyes on prey from a mile away in the air. We've been pretty well off and protected and we don't need to have any more changes." He was sure to make Shadow aware that he was willing to risk it all in order to win.

"I never asked you to speak with my company. He's like a brother to me, and if the respect is dished out to him, then it's like a slap in my face. This is my home and my operation. I make the decisions." Erica snapped her neck to the side in a disapproving manner.

Shadow smirked at the tactics Michael was trying to use against him. It was always said that if a person pulled a stunt against the ones he's close to, it'll eventually start to smell on their breath, linger on their clothes, and even show on their face.

"First off I can't remember even holding at least three conversations with you. I've never had a reason to lie. You aren't a factor in my world. Ghost and these women in this household are, and that's something you could never change. I'm here for a reason, and I don't give a damn how you felt about it." He threw up both hands with a non-caring expression.

Erica was trying to remain calm as Michael started to respond. Their pointless differences didn't give her what she needed, and going at each other's throat was only gonna force her to lash out. All her soul needed was to heal shit back together, but judging from the way the two men in front of her argued back and forth, shit was personal.

Easing down the hallway of the second floor, Tiffany stopped at everyone's room to grab all the unclean laundry. She would be heading out to show Reeses some love tonight for her initiation. She arrived in the Islands yesterday. The request for a day with her child and loving companion Stone was granted. Coming home to a loved one from behind those walls was beautiful. A foundation had been paved for her along the way, and the empty chair at their table had to be filled. No one better than her Brother Jimmie's daughter to step in, she thought before making a left on the next corner hallway.

Tiffany's feet came to halt in front of Laylah's door. She overheard her engaging in a light conversation with herself inside the room. Knowing that it was around that time of the day. She thought about her medication, and remembered that her daughter had been gone for over a few weeks. The responsibilities of taking her daily doses of depression and anger pills had more than likely been tossed to the side.

Tiffany opened the door, causing Laylah's head to jolt up from the spot she was sitting on the floor. Her Apple laptop was open, and tons of papers were scattered across the smooth carpet, as if she was looking for thirty years' worth of tax information.

"Who are you talking to?" she questioned, still holding the bucket of clothes in her arm.

Laylah pulled off her glasses with a light smile. "Mami, I was telling Dad about——"

"Laylah, your dad is gone, honey, so who could you physically be talking to? You're eighteen now, and I've explained this over and over for the past six years, baby. I know it hurts, and you have your theories on what you feel. You have to let him go from your mind, or the doctors will keep forcing me to give you the medicine." Tiffany silenced her with a pointed finger. "I love you, but I don't like when you scare me like this. You're the smartest member of this family, and I need you to act like it."

"But Mama," she tried to explain with enthusiasm pumping through her body.

"No buts, Laylah. I mean it. No more conversations to yourself, or you're taking the pills. I don't want to do this, but I can't allow you to push yourself away from me because of something you only think is real. Focus. I'm not trying to hear Erica upset more." Tiffany stared down into her daughter's matching green eyes. She was her exact replica. From face to feet, they were definitely biologically related, and the pureness that came from her skills made it positive that Chance's blood was flushing through her system daily. Her gifts were dangerous, but extraordinary at the same time.

"Yes," she agreed before removing her glasses. That familiar dark look started to form in Laylah's light eyes, and before Tiffany gave in and started to pamper her, she turned around, leaving her to grieve alone.

Closing her door, Tiffany could still hear the heated conversation that Erica was holding downstairs with Shadow and Michael. Dealing with a family criminal enterprise just didn't seem to be as peachy as a bitch would expect it to be. A person could ride along for the struggle and change when it involved either going to jail or keeping it thorough about ties with money. Her main problem was not the finances or success with their investments. It was keeping her children and Erica from going astray.

After strolling down the hall towards her washer and dryer sectional, Tiffany started a fresh load to be cleaned and took a deep breath. She couldn't help but to view herself inside of the glass mirror hanging perfectly on the wall across from her. The brown string Jimmy Choo's on her feet added a burst of flavor to the tight Milano sweatpants on her backside. She was sporting a fitted white Milano T-shirt and the long curly hair she recently dyed blonde gave her a sexier, but more dominant swag. Just looking like a top notch Queen, or having the same capabilities as one, wasn't enough for you to be fit for a throne. It took decisions, and even after wanting her dream team back for so many years, she refused to let the business fall and leave them with nothing, no matter how sad shit could ever get.

Remembering that she had to grab a gift for Reeses before the time grew late, Tiffany headed off for the room to retrieve her cell phone. Upon passing Laylah's door again, her feet stopped in place for the second time. Not only was she back talking to herself, but she was sharing a laugh at her own remarks. That was where the line had to be drawn.

Tiffany's face tightened with anger before she grabbed the knob and walked inside. The time her eyes landed on Laylah, and it felt as if her heart was seconds from liquidating through her flesh. No words could escape her lips, and she didn't want to blink out of fear of losing that special hypnotizing moment.

Laylah's head raised up from her computer with a smile deeper than the Grand Canyon. Ghost sat gently on her bed while she showed him the important research on her screen. His eyes swiftly locked in Tiffany, examining her posture and face. Tears started to fall quickly down her cheeks, but she still refused to say his name. It just couldn't be real.

"Daddy, now that Mama knows I haven't been lying this entire time, does that still make me your true savage?" She looked up at him with a precious grin.

"Of course, princess. You were always my savage, and that could never change." He spoke loud enough just for Tiffany to hear his response.

"Chance?" she whispered, placing a hand over her chest.

A finger raised up to his lips for her to remain quiet. "Shut the door," he ordered calmly.

Doing as she was told, Tiffany closed them all inside the room and stared into the face of a man she loved more than anyone could ever imagine. His hair still was wavy. His eyes still glowed with murder and misunderstanding, and the long scar on the side of his face only forced you to believe that Demonic could possibly be his first name. His style was still thuggish: a Brooklyn Nets snapback, all-black fitted Zara jeans, and a pair of low top Air Force Ones.

"I told you, Ma." Laylah giggled from the way he was staring at her mother.

Tiffany never moved an inch, nor did her eyes divert from his handsome face when he stood and crossed the small trail to be closer. Her chest felt as if a massive heart attack was approaching. Tylenol couldn't help the fact that he was trailing fingers gently down her soft, chubby cheeks, with a bright smile.

Tiffany's mind said that it was beyond a dream when his touch graced her skin. His energy was high as fuck. You could smell the Giorgio Armani fragrance floating from his skin along with a hint of exotic weed, and that small twitch in his eye let her know that Chance Grey's ass was far from fucking dead.

"Did you miss me?" He brushed his nose against hers, knowing that she was dying to feel his touch.

She was so distraught, and didn't know whether her pussy was screaming out dick or daddy. A man hadn't had the chance to receive a handshake from Tiffany since the last time Ghost touched her.

She slapped him across the right cheek. Tiffany grabbed his jawline, forcing him to witness her emotions from their suffering without him. "Where the fuck have you been? It's been ten years, Chance, and if you think about lying, you might as well walk out of my life for good."

"Laylah, do Daddy a favor and let me speak to your mama alone for a second. Take your phone and ear buds out on your patio for some music while you wait."

"Yes Daddy." She stood up immediately to follow his request after grabbing her Galaxy S10. Laylah walked to the balcony glass door in her bedroom and stepped out.

Tiffany was still cutting a crater in his face with her gorgeous eyes, and all she wanted first was her answer. Ghost changed that quickly after leaning in for a deep and long tongue kiss. Just from the way he sucked on her shit forced the madness to subside. He grabbed a handful of her ass, squeezing it with pleasure.

"First of all, I said I missed you."

Exhaling deeply to stay focused, Tiffany gazed at him. "Just tell me why so I can understand, because Chance, I really don't." She tried to keep her voice at a minimum so they wouldn't be heard.

"My father," he admitted truthfully. "Explaining it will only force you into more anger, and I didn't make it all the way down here to backtrack. I'm here to handle my business so we can be a family again. I stayed away in order to protect y'all, but the only thing that did was cause more harm to grow. I'm home now, and nothing will ever be able to make me experience that again," he stated with a positive confirmation.

Even though it wasn't the best response, it was better than none at all. Her man was still alive, and once he addressed his issue, it was final in her mind. She believed him, and whatever decision he chose to make from there was stamped.

"I missed you too, Ghost." She buried her face into his chest. Her arms rubbed up and down his back as he planted kisses on her neck and head. "We've been through some shit without you. It's just hard to believe that you're really standing right here." She rubbed two fingers through his chin hair as he held firmly on to her waist.

"It's true, but I have to make sure it stays that way. Where is Michael?" he asked, snapping back to the killer he was.

"Downstairs in the family room with Shadow and Erica. They've been arguing since he walked through the door."

"What about Mariah?" He checked the clip of his gun, sliding it back in slowly.

"Mariah is in St. Thomas. That's her station. No one else is here but the guards out front," she assured him.

Ghost nodded, sliding the pistol back on his waist. "Well, let's go." He tried to grab her hand and head out the room.

"Wait! Wait, baby, you can't just go down there like that. Erica is not gonna have the same reaction as me. Maybe you should wait until nightfall when she's asleep," Tiffany suggested with a nervous look.

Ghost chuckled. "I'm sure that she will understand as well. I can handle her. My mind is locked in on my dad. Just follow my lead, and it'll go as planned," he said before reaching for the door again.

Tiffany made one last attempt, placing a hand over his. "Please, Chance. She isn't the same sweet girl you left ten years back. Erica is dangerous, and the slightest thing can make her lash out and really hurt someone. You made a monster the day you walked out of our lives, and that was a promise she stuck with. She has literally become the reaper of these islands and carved the Grey's family name into every piece of drug that crosses our water. She's been the leader of our protection and hasn't missed a beat. If you go down there right now, chaos will quake this rock," she repeated with a hand resting on her forehead.

"Trust me. I won't allow it. Grab Laylah and tell her to come also. A family discussion is needed, and I think it's time to vote a bitch off this island," Ghost made it known before peeking out of his daughter's bedroom door.

Chapter 8

Shadow stood against the wall of Erica's living room, listening to Michael blabber about the way his son left them for dead. He chose the street rush over protection for the same grandchildren that he feels blessed to have. Nothing positive, not even a simple remark of love for the same seed who placed him back in position after Jesus's critical punishment.

Erica was tired of hearing the bashing and criticism against anybody sharing the same blood with the Grey family. The Ramirez name was more praised through his lips, and the hatred was quite evident. She couldn't hold it in any longer. "Why the fuck did you come here if this family only has so much foundation to stand on? Seems like the only time you do respect us is when you're here alone or involved with a half a million dollar transaction. You never speak greatness about us, or even try to motivate anyone within this operation to remain firm with loyalty for your son even after he's been gone. This is what he built, but something is telling me that you really wished that it could've been you to win. It didn't happen that way." Erica shook her head before folding her arms. "Chance did it without you and without a team of dick riders and family who only scheme for a loved one's demise. The Grey s are self-sufficient, and these islands belong to our side, not the Ramirez's."

The way Michael sat on the couch toying with the sleeves of his collared shirt made it seem like her statements were obsolete. No one attempted to discover all the work Michael placed in for Jesus, but the known hatred for his own three grandchildren trashed all hopes of being the star and leader for the Ramirez bloodline. Jesus ignited a fire with the disrespect for his son's children and made sure that they all would be denied any access to their powerful resources. That disagreement started about old funds that were past due. Once he didn't receive a fair exchange for his work, he made a choice that would create a lifetime of deadly confusion.

"I couldn't care less how you fucking feel. Of course my family was better. We created the way. Remember? Sucks that I had to lose all I've built because I wanted to fuck a few of you black losers, but what's done is done. Everyone makes a bed, darling. You just have to be prepared to sleep in it after. You're right, I'm here to make money, live life, and have the things I never got a chance to. I'm not here for emotions and time wasting about how powerful I can make this organization. I'm just doing it."

"Well, I guess you just happened to fall into the wrong two black bitch's pussies, because the two that run this household will always praise the king of our throne. That ain't you, and it never will be." Erica ice grilled him as the venomous feelings rolled off her tongue.

Michael took the backlash like a champ and smiled. It was true that when a bitch got in her feelings, you would be able to feel it crying from their skin. In his eyes, that's all she was: a dumb bitch who was given some authority.

Shadow's head rose when he spotted Ghost, Laylah, and Tiffany walk smoothly into the kitchen without being noticed. Michael was so focused on the response that he never noticed Ghost standing in his presence until they locked eyes. His body tensed with adrenaline from the cold look on his face.

"Whatever the fuck you have to say is not acceptable on the grounds of my home. We react from actions, and every order I make on this territory will be handled successfully. Do us a favor and try not to help," Erica spat before noticing that Michael's attention was elsewhere.

Laylah strolled further inside, passing Erica. "Hey Ma." She kissed her cheek before taking a seat next to her grandfather.

"Hey princess. Where did you come from?" Her question faded off as the hairs on her arms began to rise. She looked from Michael over to Shadow's clueless face. She glanced behind her before slowly turning to face the reason it all fell.

Tiffany and Ghost stood no more than fifteen feet away from her. His gaze acknowledged her sincerely, but his vision remained sealed on Michael.

Erica squinted her eyes at him before placing a hand over her mouth. Dark flashes of their past started to rush through her brain as she opened her palm, reaching out for him. Being sure not to approach her too fast, Ghost took a small step forward and witnessed the look in her eyes switch from hurt to death in a matter of seconds. Snatching the pistol from her holster, she placed it directly on his forehead.

"Tell me you're not real, motherfucker. All you have to do is speak so I can know!" she yelled at the top of her lungs. Veins were bulging from her neck, and the hand she used to grip her weapon was clenched tighter than a rusted bolt.

"I know it may be hard right now, but I prepared myself for accepting whatever you choose after I explain," Ghost spoke humbly before she pulled back the hammer.

"Erica, please!" Tiffany stammered, trying not to cry again. She could tell that Laylah was getting confused from the reactions of everyone in the room. The last thing she needed was a mishap with a violent person, and her mind could only process so much before moving off impulse. "Baby, just calm down and let him talk. He's here. This is what you wanted. Don't end it like this. Please?" she begged with both hands held out in front of her.

"Mama, what's going on?" Laylah's chest heaved as she looked over at Tiffany.

"Baby girl, nothing is going on. Just sit back down and relax. Daddy is just trying to get things squared away to bring this family back together. Isn't that right, Erica?" she asked to see if her head was still trying to function.

Shadow stood back, hoping that her finger didn't graze that trigger. His mind was thinking of a plan to calm the aura of the house down, but if someone snapped too soon, he would probably be carrying Ghost, or another member of their family, out under a sheet.

As the last tear dropped from her right eye, Erica turned her weapon around, aiming for Michael's head. Before he could blink, a bullet escaped from the back of her chamber, colliding into his forehead.

Boom! The loud eruption froze the entire living room for a second.

Ghost didn't blink or even flinch at the sight of his father's body sliding down the couch, but he knew that the reaction was about to cause the biggest catastrophe the Grey family has ever seen.

"Papa!" Laylah screamed in horror before reaching for her own pistol.

Shadow quickly tackled her to the ground before she could remove it from her waistline and Erica didn't hesitate to turn back around and shove the barrel of her gun back into Ghost's face. "That was for him lying to me. Now give me another excuse to prove that you're standing right here!" Her eyes continued to flutter with anger.

Ghost exhaled gently and tried his best to slash Laylah's screams from his ears. "As I said, I'm home, baby. The excuses are irrelevant. What's next?" He crossed his hands calmly as if that was the last statement he had to offer.

Tiffany's chest heaved up and down. She wondered what was about to occur next because losing their love after it took so long for him to return was going to crush the spirits of everyone when they got the news of what was taking place in the mansion.

A few of Erica's armed guards slowly entered the living room area with their guns in hand just in case she gave them the word to kill. Her finger trickled across the trigger. She wanted to pull away, but her mind just couldn't allow her to. Once the gun lowered down to her side, she let out an exhausted sigh. "I'll see you two in the room. You have five minutes, or when I come back out, I'm killing the both of you!" she yelled with a sinister look at Ghost and Tiffany before walking off towards the master bedroom.

Ghost looked around at the armed Jamaicans and popped his neck from side to side. "So this went differently than I expected."

"I warned you!" Tiffany snapped before grabbing Laylah from Shadow's arms. "We have to go in there, or she is coming back out on a rampage."

Ghost ignored her anger with a slick smile. Kissing his daughter's forehead, he gazed down into her eyes. "Your papa was trying to hurt Daddy, Laylah, which means he was not a part of us. I want you to snap back and calm down. Listen to me," he whispered into her ear.

The shakiness in her body slowly began to ease, and the tears that flowed down her face immediately stopped before she wrapped her arms around his neck. Ghost patted her back as Tiffany mugged him

"Shadow, please keep an eye on her until me and Tiffany can resolve this issue with my new lunatic. Whatever happens is gonna determine how we move from here, because there is surely animosity heading our way about the clown she just murdered," he stated while glancing at the large bullet hole in Michael's head.

"You don't say?" Shadow huffed, shaking his head.

Looking at Tiffany, Ghost held out his hand for her to grab. Once she accepted, he walked slowly through the bottom hallway until they reached Erica's master bedroom. Turning the knob, Ghost stepped inside first.

Standing by her queen-size Italian made bed, her naked body glowed with perfection. Her long hair was hanging gently down her back, and her Hershey brown irises were locked in on them as if she was ready to attack at any second. The pistol dangling from her right hand indicated that she was far from done with her mission, and it was clearly exciting to Ghost from the way he smirked at her feistiness.

"No one has ever made me feel like him. From a kiss down to his touch. No man has touched my body since he's been gone. If you're Ghost like you say, make love to me, because if you're not, and this is some type of trick or nightmare, I'll blow your brains out before you can take a second pump in my pussy," she threatened clutching the gun tightly.

Tiffany gave him a look that said he was on his own with the psychopathic nutcase he created. After ten years of dealing with her aggressiveness, it was time for him to witness that scar he engraved the day he disappeared.

Nodding humbly, Ghost took off his hat and slid the T-shirt from over his head, tossing it to the side. His chiseled chest was bulky, showing off his large abs, and a few war scars were visible on the side of his rib cage. He eased slowly over to her while unbuttoning his Zara jeans and dropping them to the floor.

Erica's eyes roamed his body up and down as he got closer, and Ghost could feel her sexual tension rising with every step he made. By the time he reached her, his hands were eager to grab a hold of her immaculate body. Her pussy was waxed to perfection, and her breasts were sitting up perfectly as if they were begging for his lips to douse them with pleasure.

Erica slid down on the bed with her eyes never leaving his. He couldn't help but to lick his lips at the new thickness she had developed since his departure. He dropped his Calvin Klein boxer briefs to the floor and his dick flopped out like an angry midget man swinging.

Tiffany removed her clothes slowly, but refused to rush over in case the worst was about to occur. Once Ghost crawled down between her legs, Erica placed her gun to his temple.

"Try me," she mumbled with her bottom lip shaking profusely.

"I love you." Ghost nodded, licking the base of his fingers.

He slid them across her kitty lips. He wasted no time easing his large manhood inside right after. The first stroke he delivered forced her eyes to roll in euphoria. Erica's wetness began to slowly drizzle out, and by the time Ghost made his second deep trail between her thighs, her pussy sounded off with delight. Old memories of their past began to flush through her system. The way he catered to their every need. The way his mind stopped at nothing to ensure their greatness. The sad moments, down to the critical ones of even saving her life from their sworn enemies. It was a rush that nearly caused her heart to burst, and when she opened her eyes, the first orgasm from his hypnotizing dick game spilled recklessly from her sweet spot. The gun in her hand fell to the floor, and her eyes began to tear up immediately

."Chance?" she whispered, placing a hand on his cheek bone.

"Yes." He smiled seductively, feeling her insides become stickier.

"Oh my Goddd," she panted when he started to long stroke her pussy viciously. Erica's nails lodged into his back, and she opened her legs wider, feeling his shit touch the bottom of her honeypot.

After the next five minutes of applying seducing pleasure to the pussy that was rightfully his, he gazed down into her eyes before busting his seed into her womb.

Erica's wild ride of satisfaction began to slowly decrease, and a wicked smile formed across her face. "Welcome home, daddy," she panted before kissing his lips aggressively.

Ghost couldn't help but to grin at the new woman that had transitioned from his gullible sweetheart. Her entire aura proclaimed her to be a true boss, the queen of his throne, and he was enjoying every second of it.

Erica stepped out of the bed and glanced back at him before heading towards the bathroom. "Just so you know, all of this that you see is what I've built since you've been away. These islands belong to me, and I'm glad that you can finally come and assist me with my empire."

Ghost laid his back against the silk pillow on the bed with a raised eyebrow. "Nah, you must have forgotten. This shit belongs to me, and I'm glad to be back home where you can follow my lead as you should."

"That's right, daddy." She snickered before walking smoothly into the master bathroom for a shower.

Ghost eyes moved over to Tiffany standing at the side of his bed naked. Her fingers fiddled lightly against the skin of her folded arms nervously as his eyes molested her thickness. "Do I have to come get it?" he questioned, showing his manhood, which was rising back up while he spoke.

Tiffany's eyes glowed in delight knowing that shit was far beyond real. It was officially confirmed that the man of their home was back, and he was taking his spot by force. The Grey family was reunited, she thought before jumping under the covers with the animal she had desired for the past decade.

Chris Green

Chapter 9

Stepping out of the airport doors, Frost and Eva made their way towards the six parked GMC Terrains. The fresh island smell was like heaven to her nostrils. Tourists moved around as if they were in paradise. The leaves on the trees, down to the beautiful tulip flowers, made her realize that it was such a joy to have eyes around every part of the United States soil. Death was on her mind, and what better place to acquire such feelings than the tropical Virgin Islands? Looking at her aunt end the phone call she was currently indulged in allowed her to ask the question that had been eating at her since they received the call she waited so patiently for.

"Now that we're down here on this little rock, are you gonna tell me this secret little snitch who's giving you this information? How can we even be sure that it's accurate and this isn't a wasted trip?" she questioned as their guards stood around with eagle eyes on everyone that strolled past them.

Eva smiled before applying a small amount of red cherry gloss to her lips. "Because, dear. The chief of police has allowed us a few weeks of destruction. The little rabbit has stopped down here, which means your little papi is trying to come back out of hiding. This is your time, love. Your fun may begin." She nodded in approval.

Frost grinned from ear to ear like a spoiled kid on Christmas day. Opening one of the back doors of her security's truck, she removed a mini carbon 15 semi-automatic with a seventy five round drum. Racking the chamber back, she aimed at the walking tourists laughing hysterically and started to let loose as if July 4th was coming around for a second time of the year.

Boom! Boom! Boom! Boom! Boom! Boom! Boom! Boom! Boom!

Eva smirked as the large crowds started to disperse like a group of lions attacking a pack of sheep. Screams erupted from the ones getting struck by Frost's loose bullets, and the smell of fresh blood enticed her. The hunt for Chance Grey was on, and she didn't mind breezing through every inch of the islands until they were able to cross each other's paths for the last encounter of war.

* * *

Walking out of his bathroom, Ghost dusted off his new light brown Sinola collared shirt. The tannish color matched his Valentino slacks and crispy Mayson Mariela dress shoes. An Audemers watch was sported on his right wrist, and his hair was freshly washed, showing the spin in his thick waves. The smell of Yves Saint Laurent emanated from his skin, causing Erica's head to drift around with a wide smile when he entered the living room.

"Hey sexy." She moved towards him and kissed his lips like an innocent little girl who was meeting her prom date. Her anger had finally been replaced with happiness after Ghost finally settled back into his rightful position on the throne.

"Wassup, love?" He pinched her butt with his strong right hand and glanced around at everyone else.

Shadow, Tiffany, Laylah, and a few of Erica's henchmen sat around the living room wondering what the next move was for the boss of Savages now that he was back home.

"Where is Mariah?"

"She's in St. Thomas. That's her designated spot. We all have an assigned space in order to keep our product, and press down to ensure no one gets over. Since you've been gone, we've managed to get the entire Virgin Islands, including Jamaica, thanks to our Puerto Rican connections. We have ties down through Florida and even Haiti," Tiffany informed him with confidence, knowing that he would be more than proud of how they handled the family's foundation.

"Really? So who's running Jamaica? Because that's a major distance away from here, and those aren't the nicest slums to play around?"

"Reeses's daddy. She just took her position after getting out of the Feds a few days ago.

Ghost's heart stumbled hearing her name. "Reeses?"

"Yes, your magnificent niece has finally stepped into her Grey family bloodline, and she is over in Jamaica. Her welcome warming party is tonight," Erica confirmed.

"Take me to her now!" Ghost ordered.

"As you wish." She grabbed her cell to place a call.

* * *

Kingston, Jamaica
The Slums

After the relaxing and smooth four hour ride on the massive Yamaha speed boat, the Grey family had finally arrived on the dangerous turf of Jamaica. The sun was sliding down past the horizon on the coast, and Ghost had to admit, nothing felt more important than having his family beside him at the moment. Every few seconds he would glance over at Erica and Tiffany, who sat in their own little section cuddling like the best friends of the world. Their bond was so amazing. The love was pure, and he could definitely tell that it was way tighter than the one he left ten years ago. Shadow was sitting in the back with his arms folded, enjoying the wind as it wisped through his hair. He was still the same: the funny friend that was also dangerous, and truthful about every step that he made. Everything he'd offered to Ghost was nothing but sincere and he had genuine love for a homie that couldn't be replaced by anyone on his team. After all the time of staying away from Michael for the safety of his girls, he knew that the right sign would eventually be shown to let him know when it was the moment to make his presence back known.

Laylah was posted right at Ghost's side as usual. His daddy instincts told him that things were only settled for now, but his princess was the key to a bigger mission. She was the inner beast for their bloodline, and regardless of who felt differently, Laylah was gonna become the leader of the Grey family one day. He still had yet to surprise his oldest baby girl Mariah with his return. She was grounded on keeping the family's finances coming in by the second, and that was surely the only way their generations could thrive for the long run.

Once the speedboat pulled up next to the private dock, you could see the large fire canister sticks that were lit aligning the pathway. Numerous armed Rasta's were lined across the platform, holding guns that could split a great white shark in half if fired off. Erica was the first one to stand and exit the boat when it came to a complete halt. A guard assisted her with a helping hand until her white heels touched the flattop. Her body was wrapped in a tight, spaghetti-strapped Dries Van Noten dress showing off her amazing figure, and her hair was pinned in a double bun with a light coat of makeup applied to her gorgeous face. Laylah and Tiffany followed directly behind her, exiting off the motor boat with the same assistance she received.

As Ghost stepped off next with Shadow behind him, a guard touched his chest aggressively. "You get searched, mon! Spread ya hands." He waved the gun recklessly as if he was ready to pop some shit.

Pushing his hand down, Ghost barked loudly. "Never put ya hands on me unless you trying to be shitting in yo' pants and taking ya last breath, fuckas!"

Everybody paused to look back, but the guard spoke before Erica could make a statement. "Nuttin' happenin' without the boss lady's word, pussyhole!" His accent grew thicker.

Quickly slapping the barrel of the gun from his face, Ghost delivered a hard right fist to his jaw, shattering his shit to pieces. Once his backside hit the boardwalk, he removed his pearl handled Glock 40 and placed two hot slugs through the center of his nasal cavity.

Before the other guards could lift their weapons, Erica snapped her fingers twice. "If you motherfuckers even have the nerve to raise a gun at my King, you'll be crocodile food before morning. I know what you all have been used to, but things have slightly changed in the past few hours. This is Ghost, and if you value your life, you all will show him the same respect as you do to me," she ordered, continuing up the walkway.

Shadow leaned closer to Ghost, whispering in his ear after realizing how much power Erica really possessed. "She's like Queen fucking Elizabeth down here." He chuckled.

"Shut the fuck up, idiot! That nigga just like to made me spazz out and empty my clip on all these bitches," Ghost huffed before wiping the speck of blood that had splattered on his cheek.

A few of the guards picked up the dead body of the slain Jamaican, and tossed him directly into the water. Most of them lowered their vision as Ghost started to move past them.

"Just to inform all y'all on what's going on, since my woman has more fear instilled in you pussies than me. I'm the boss of this shit now, and when I move, niggas freeze. Do I make myself clear?" He stared around at all the quiet men.

"Ya, bad mon, we hear ya, boss." One of the men nodded with his hands clasped together.

"Good." He walked off with Shadow following his trail until they caught up with everyone else.

Ghost grabbed ahold of Erica's and Tiffany's hands as they continued up the neatly carved dirt path flowers aligned on the sides. Reggae music could be heard pumping through a set of speakers, and by the time their feet hit the curb of the dangerous property, everything came to life. Tons of masked women danced throughout the street with a line of reggae drummers standing to the side beating their hands across the solid instruments. The echo of loud shouting could be heard as different groups of men tangoed with some of the most gorgeous women Ghost had ever laid his eyes on. It was like one huge block party. A variety of Caribbean food was stationed around the area, the scent of it lingering through the air. A small parade of twerk dancers held the middle of the street, performing to the beat. It was like a live Miami club that only hosted outside events for the freakiest people on the large island.

Erica walked through the crowds with Ghost and Tiffany directly beside her. The people on the pathway parted for them like the Red Sea with every step they took, and once their presence crossed the street where the large group of Trench Town Killa's stood heavily, Ghost's eyes landed on Reeses, who sat on the hood of a 2019 Jeep Wrangler Rubicon. A giant ganja wrap was in between her fingers, and a bottle of White Remy sat in between her legs. A Green MCM dress was fitted to perfection on her hypnotizing body, offsetting the black Frances Valentine heels on her feet, and her jet black hair was braided straight to the back with a yellow ribbon lacing through the amazing design in her scalp. She bobbed gently to the beat until her chief bodyguard and husband Stone tapped her leg with his finger, pointing at the family.

Turning her attention towards Erica and Tiffany she smiled, but had to do a double take at the man who stood between them. His appearance may have changed slightly, but his smile was one that she could never forget. With Stone's help, she slid off the hood of her car and moved slowly towards them. The slow pace Reeses started off with turned into her running like a small child until she was able to jump into his arms.

"Oh my God! Uncle Ghost?" she uttered with a hand on his cheek.

Tiffany couldn't help but to grin from her reaction. It had been years since their bond was kindled together, and the thought of Jimmie smiling down on them both caused her heart to pump tears of joy. It was truly a miracle that had finally been answered. The bloodline was reunited.

"Hey, little one. Did you count me out on that promise I made?" Ghost asked with a wide smile.

"Not for one second. Everyone told me that you were dead. I like the cool scar." She giggled, rubbing a finger across his wound.

"I think it fits me too. You've grown up wonderful, baby girl, and I'm glad to see you've made your way down here where you belong. With us."

"This is like a real episode of family matters." Shadow chuckled, bobbing to the reggae beat.

As everyone vibed and enjoyed that sacred moment, Laylah removed her holstered pistol when she noticed a large group of suited law officials quickly making their way through the block party. "Mama," she alerted, nudging Tiffany's arm.

Ghost, Shadow, and Erica turned around just in time as General Cannon, the lieutenant of the Jamaican military, trailed through their event. The armed guards blocked off their path before they could reach the Grey family, causing Erica to wave her hand for the music to cease. Once the silence filled the air, the only sound heard was a small mumble of, "No apologies."

General Cannon raised his hand for his men to stay put as he moved forward. His eyes locked in on Erica as he removed his uniform hat. "Ms. Grey, I know that this is an unexpected pop up, but it's a must that I speak with you," he requested in his thick accent.

Erica stepped forward with Ghost and the family directly by her side. "This is a family gathering, and you've tarnished it already, so you should already be speaking General Cannon. I pray that it's important, because this is a moment that you will not be able to replace," she threatened indirectly

"Yes ma'am. A terrible situation has broken out in the Virgin Islands. Today there was a massive shooting at the airport leaving eight civilians dead and thirteen critically injured. At first we thought that this was a terrorist attack upon the island, but after a few hours of investigation, we see that our theory was very incorrect."

"I pay you a million dollars a month to tell me accurate information, not riddles. What does this have to do with me?"

General Cannon nodded before swallowing the spit in his throat. "Ms. Grey, the assault was made by two women. These two individuals stated to one of my wounded officers that they were here in search of you. 'Death to the Grey family' was their specific words. Their current location is St. John, and I'm not positive on what exact motive these people have in mind, but since their arrival, there have been four more deaths on that island alone. I'm not positive how you are trying to proceed with this, but they aren't alone," he explained with grief and worry in his tone.

"What? Is this some type of joke?" Erica closed the distance between them so she could look directly into his eyes.

"No ma'am. She was sure to leave her name and make it known that you and your family's blood is on a timeline. "General Cannon quickly dug in his pocket, removing a small piece of paper and handing it over to her.

Erica snatched the information, and paused upon seeing the name. She looked back at Ghost with a stunned expression. She mumbled her name with a face of hatred. "Eva."

Ghost grabbed Tiffany's hand, forcing her to look at him. "Get everyone back to the house. We need to secure the family now. Everyone, including Mariah," he authorized, waving for Reeses and Laylah to stay close to her. "Get someone to hold down the position in Jamaica until we find this bitch. I'm not risking anyone being separated again."

Erica was so distraught that all she could do was stand still with a speechless face. Ghost rubbed a hand across her cheek snapping the trance away quickly. "Baby, I need you to stay focused. We're going back to the mansion. I need to explain what's next so we're all on the same page. Do you understand?"

"Yes." She nodded, holding his arm, feeling that the destruction was igniting back up again.

Ghost walked over to General Cannon with Shadow moving directly behind him. "I'm not sure if you know who I am, but that isn't important because you'll see that I let my actions speak for itself. How much time do I have to wreck these islands and find this bitch before a higher authority gets involved?"

Cannon looked back at Erica, who nodded in approval before answering. "One week. My connections can only hold so much weight, and I can assist with a few of my men. Ms. Grey is the only reason I'm in the seat I sit in today so my gratitude and respect goes far for the family, sir. But if these people aren't caught for the slayings of those innocent lives, the Federal Bureau of Investigation will take positions over those islands within nine days or less. I pray that you have a game plan good enough to place an end to this."

"Leave that to me." Ghost grabbed Erica's hand and started to make his way back towards the boat dock with the entire family right beside them. He knew that the time would eventually present itself when that spiteful and conniving bitch would surface, but there was one difference now. Making it out alive from his grasp wasn't gonna be an option. She would die slowly or miserably.

A set of eyes watched from the far back crowd as things started to disperse. The stubby blunt that burned between his lips was tossed to the ground before he removed his cell phone and placed a call.

"Well hello. Torey." Eva's sweet voice spoke through the line.

"You can proceed. He knows."

"Good. I'll start with his oldest daughter first. Remember that you aren't the only hungry child that wants his head, so have patience. It'll be more than worth it." She snickered evilly.

"I'm keeping an eye on your general. I have nothing but time, Auntie." He grinned before hanging up.

Chapter 10
Florida State Prison
Starke, Florida

The guard fumbled lightly with his keys as he headed for the small holding tank to process the rest of the release papers for his last inmate of the day. The rundown penitentiary was on its last leg. He used his walkie talkie to have the cell popped open since the key wasn't sufficient to handle the objective at the time.

"Cell 220," he spoke clearly into the device.

Seconds later a loud buzz erupted, allowing the door to swing open. Once his eyes landed on the man inside, he shook his head at the demon that the state was allowing to step back into society. The charges on his rap sheet alone made his skin crawl.

"Mr. Rico, seems that you've been granted access to commit more fuckery in the United States. I've got thirty minutes before I get out of this shithole job. Where do you want your bus ticket?" the agitated guard asked before slapping the two hundred dollar check into his right palm.

"I don't want a bus ticket. I need a plane."

"A plane. Well, where in the fuck are you trying to go, fella?"

"To the Virgin Islands." He cracked a wry smile.

* * *

The Grey mansion

A light mist of rain was drizzling from the sky and tapping gently against the windows of Ghost's mansion. He moved around, explaining to the thirty armed guards in his living room the new update for patrolling the perimeter. There were over forty men stationed around the barriers of the beach, then six men kept watch on the roof, and the rest that were standing in his presence were ordered to walk the area for a six hour shift before switching out with replacements to ensure that his girls were secured.

Erica sat on the couch with her legs crossed, sipping on a flute filled with gold chardonnay. The thought of Eva having enough guts to make a move against her after Ghost's return only meant that she was truly trying to die, so talking wasn't really on her agenda at the time. Tiffany held the seat next to her as Laylah and Shadow stood around waiting for the next response on what they needed to do.

Ghost thought before he spoke and pointed at Laylah. "Call Mariah back. Why isn't she here yet?" he asked with aggravation.

"I told her twice, Daddy. She wanted you to know that she's not going against your word, but her guards are keeping her well secured, and the business she's handling won't be finished until early in the a.m. She said it would be a better time for her to move when the sun's out."

"Call her." He ignored her reply, folding his arms.

Laylah used the IM chatting app to video her, and once her face appeared on the screen, she placed it in her father's hand.

"Hey Daddy." Mariah smiled staring into his eyes.

"I thought I said that it was mandatory to be at the house so we all can be stationed together, baby girl. You know that this woman is out here lurking, and I'm not willing to take any chances." He gave her a look of disappointment.

"I know, Dad. But you know how I am about business. I'm wrapping up the count and transactions for the connections in Tivoli Gardens and Haiti, plus I have over fifty men around me with guns 24/7. I can fight against President Trump if I have to. I promise that I can make it before eight in the morning. It's better to move during daylight anyway."

"Are you sure?" He gazed at her on the cell phone screen, feeling that she wasn't positive.

"Yes, papa bear. It's great to see you. Now go and have some fun with the family, and let's worry about this minor problem tomorrow. We own these islands, remember?" Her smile forced him to grin from ear to ear.

True enough. Eva was a major problem, but Mariah was right. There wasn't a space on the island they couldn't reach, and before the bitch-ass aunt of his made any severe move against them, she would be slipping in a pile of her own blood. He had put the memo out that he wanted her dead or alive. It was now only a matter of time before she was making her pledge to God.

"Okay, baby girl, but please make sure you're here bright and early. No exceptions," Ghost gave in.

"I love you so much, Daddy," she said as if it was the last time she'd see him again before ending the video chat.

Ghost handed the phone back to Laylah. He smiled and rubbed both hands across his face. "Listen, I know that this filthy fish-smelling bitch is trying to make a so-called plot against us, but I'm not gonna let that shit kill our joy. It's been a long time since I been home, and we should be enjoying ourselves instead of allowing this Jeepers Creepers-looking motherfucker to make us all upset." Ghost clasped his hands together with excitement.

"That's how I feel, Daddy," Laylah said with excitement.

"See, that's my baby. Grab us some champagne and glasses, baby girl."

Ghost watched his daughter run off for the kitchen. He looked at Shadow. "Dawg, you know damn well we haven't smoked a blunt in a decade. Twist us some, and let's hit this floor like we back in Atlanta, nigga."

"Hold up, hold up, folk." Shadow laughed. "I got good weed, but I was never a damn dancer. That was all you, Usher." He dug in his bag sitting against the wall and pulled out an ounce of exotic weed he copped from the dispensary shop earlier.

Ghost walked over to the large entertainment center and glanced at the iPad that was hooked up to the Sony Stereo set. Scrolling through the music log, he spotted Mary J. Blige's name and clicked on her album *Share my World*. As her single "Everything" came blaring through the speakers, he turned around and looked at Tiffany.

"Wassup, Tiff? Come vibe with me." He waved his hands in the air with a big smile.

She couldn't help but to grin from ear to ear as he moved towards her, snapping his fingers and grooving like Martin Lawrence on his late 90's TV show. "Boy, you silly as hell. You know I can't dance, Ghost." She giggled, taking his hand, and sliding out in the center of their gigantic living room.

Erica even had to share a smile as she cut her eyes over at them. The recent news about Eva still had her fuming, but of course, you could leave it up to her crazy but free-spirited lover to make them laugh.

Laylah moved back through the living area with four cold glasses of Patron and lemons on ice. She handed all of the adults on the floor one. She jumped on the couch with Erica and started to finish the recent novel she had begun typing on her iPhone about the chemistry of humans. That was enough alcohol for her.

Shadow sparked the blunt and nearly coughed up his lungs from the show Tiffany and Ghost were putting on. The atmosphere of the room went from killer instinct to happy family reunion as Mary's voice pumped through the speakers.

"You take me awa-yyyyy…from the pain, and you bring me paradise, and when I was downnn…happpyy daysss.You brought sunshine in my lifeee. It never occuredddd to me, every time I saw your face, I would fall so deep in love. That ya love can't be replacedddd…Youuu are myyyy…everything."

Ghost spun Tiffany around as if they were having the first dance and date of their life. She nearly wanted to shed a tear at the warm energy he was pushing out. The man who was standing in front of her was usually ruthless 24/7. Now his affectionate side was pouring from his spirit, showing that he truly missed his family.

Ghost was cheesing like a high school quarterback who needed his cheerleaders, and he was doing whatever to keep the vibe going. Grooving over to Erica, he rubbed a hand down her smooth thigh and flicked his tongue seductively. "Come on, baby. Kick shit with us," he said before accepting the blunt of weed from Shadow.

"I don't dance, Chance." She sipped her drink with a sexy smirk.

"Ahh, you a party pooper, fathead." He chuckled, still stepping smoothly to the beat of the R & B queen.

After ten minutes of seeing everybody laughing, high, and having fun, the small smiles that Erica shared was turning into frowns. Her leg was starting to shake with aggravation, and the irises of her eyes were starting to flush crimson red. The liquor that was settling in her system was starting to activate, and before she could stop herself, she was slinging the drinking glass in her hand across the room, causing it to shatter against the wall causing everyone to freeze in place. Her hands were trembling with anger, and Ghost could see that she wasn't in her normal zone forcing him to cut the music down.

Folding his arms humbly, he exhaled. "What's wrong, ma?"

Instead of answering him, a trail of tears began to fall down her cheeks before she stood up off the couch and stormed out of the glass patio door, closing it behind her.

Tiffany looked at Ghost and shrugged lightly. She knew that even questioning Erica about her angry outburst could lead to her being checked out or having a gun pulled, so running behind her was damn sure out of the question.

"I think this shit with Eva is really eating at her, dawg. She just got a miracle getting you back, and now it seems like the bullshit is stirring back up. It's my island regardless of how long we've been away. It's kind of easy to read her, bro. I'll leave that to you," Shadow said calmly before passing him the last of their second blunt of weed.

Ghost nodded and pulled lightly on the exotic before flashing a fake smile. "Y'all keep enjoying y'all selves. I'll go talk to her." He waved his hand, walking out of the patio door.

The drizzle from earlier had come to a halt and was replaced with a mild cool breeze. Three of the Jamaican guards saluted Ghost with a nod, but continued their patrol as he stepped out on the back deck of his home. Looking around the large patio, he spotted Erica standing at a distance down by the beach shore. He removed his designer shoes and walked through the soft sand until he reached the bottom of the beach. As he got closer, Ghost realized that she was still crying. Placing a hand at the small of her back, he rubbed it gently.

"I know that this little problem with Eva is bothering you, ma, but I can promise that she's gonna be handled," he spoke sincerely.

Erica laughed through her shedding tears. "Fuck Eva. I could care less about her because it's only a matter of time before she's split like a fucking salmon patty on my territory. I'm hurt because of your lies, Chance."

Ghost flashed a curious expression, wondering what the fuck he could've possibly lied about.

Reeses and Stone pacing along the beach caused him to pause his statement.

"Hey, Uncle Ghost. Are we discussing the new agenda yet?"

"Nah, muffin. Y'all enjoy your private time together, and we will all speak in about an hour or so." He nodded positively.

"Sure thing. Love you guys," Reeses replied and then she continued to walk along the shore with her husband.

"Always," Ghost added before stepping in front of Erica. Her beautiful black hair blew gently with the wind, and her mocha brown eyes beamed at him with a mixture of love and hatred. He could tell that she was truly furious from how the air puffed inside of her fluffy cheeks. "Excuse me, ma'am, but I'm lost. What did I lie to you about?"

"What haven't you lied to me about?" She stepped closer to him with her arms folded.

He huffed, trying not to choke the shit out of her. "I'm not sure, Erica. How about you try refreshing me a little, baby? We were all just fine. I'm not understanding?"

"Ever since we first met, I had dreams of being the best wife to you. I followed all the rules, stayed in line, and tended to all your needs and wants. I thought that giving my life to you meant things would change, Chance. I lost my career, my identity. I've lost my fucking soul for the sake of what you stood for, bae. I've even accepted the fact of another woman and another child to ensure that I can still hold you close to me. Everyone is bouncing around happy with life and your actions, and we still possess everything that you've given, but love always lost, Chance. I've lost every time you've promised me something. Tiffany is happy because she has a reason to be. Even after ten years, she's still held on to all the things you've given. Laylah has grown to be big and beautiful. Her man is back home, and anything she's wanted from miscellaneous to significant has been granted since we've all intertwined this relationship." Erica's voice trailed off before she wiped the tears off her face.

He knew that she was referring to their son Bernard. He exhaled with a sigh of empathy for his queen. "You miss him." His eyes were downcast with a sound of pain sewn through the center of his question.

Her eyes began to pour even harder. "I never even had a moment to see him have his first birthday, Chance." She buried her head inside of his chest.

Ghost couldn't help but to feel her message, because there were endless nights he pondered on how his son would have turned out for the family. There were disturbing images of his fate flashing before his mind, but he still kept the main agenda on his mind. To change his horrible demeanor and actions for the sake of his life, and loved ones now that he was back, but in order to see it prevail. He needed two more pieces deleted: Eva and Frost.

Ghost kissed Erica's lips softly and lifted her chin where she could look directly into his soul when he spoke. "I know that we've taken losses, and it may seem like you've been defeated, but God had a better plan for you, baby. He took Bernard, forced you to suffer and experience a lot of things, because you were the only one who could bear such pain. You are a survivor and warrior for him, and he knew for sure that if Tiffany or anyone else in this bloodline was placed through what you've seen, they would've broken to pieces a long time ago. You took a hold of this family. Ran the business for a decade, and with an iron fist, ma. That's the reason why no one can sit on your throne. You were made for sacrifices and strength, and you prove that every day. Just take a look around at what you're built." He spoke with encouragement.

Erica knew that his words had to be true because she never heard the man she loved so much speak on God, let alone having faith in him, or anyone else. The years he spent away definitely placed a change on his heart, and she could tell from the way his eyes sparkled with light instead of the normal darkness that lingered in him throughout the day when he was around others. It was only a safeguard for protecting the family, and if his heartless ass could try to change it up for the better, then she could too.

"I understand, and I'm glad to have you back beside me." She accepted his powerful speech and tickled her fingers through his thick waves.

"That's my boo-thang." He smiled, grabbing a handful of her plump backside.

"You better stop if you ain't tryna handle that business right here, daddy." Her eyes got low with a yearning lust.

"Okay, okay, I'ma let ya have that for now until this little meeting with everyone passes. Remember that we gotta lay beside each other tonight." He grabbed her hand and headed back up to the crib.

"You say that like I ain't got Tiffany to back me up."

"So y'all jumping now." He smiled

"Hell yeah, just for yo' ass," she replied, sharing a laugh with her King.

After making it back in the house, Reeses', Stone's, Shadow's, and Tiffany's eyes rotated straight over to them after crossing the threshold. Laylah was sitting on the floor, and jumped to her feet and embraced Erica with a tight hug.

"It's okay, Mama. I'll take care of that old lady for you," she said with a bright smile.

Ghost couldn't help but to laugh. "What the hell y'all been in here telling my daughter? I hope y'all thought of some good strategies so I can rest this big-ass mind of mine."

"Actually we have, dawg," Shadow said with all seriousness.

As Ghost and Erica took a seat on the couch, he grabbed the rolled cigar of marijuana from the table and sparked it. "So let's hear it."

Reeses stood up with a look of confidence. "I called in a few people to help us. They should be here by morning."

"Good. What else?"

Shadow smiled. "Your phantom is on the way also."

Ghost sat up slowly with a look of disbelief. "He's out?"

"Yep." Shadow grabbed the blunt from his hand.

Chapter 11

Beads of sweat dripped down Mariah's forehead as Frost and Eva sat around her basement with their newly-recruited Jamaican team. It was tough trying to make their way inside the trenches of St. Thomas where her mini mansion was stationed, but of course there was nothing a few hundred thousand couldn't finesse the poverty-bound men to do. Apparently the miserly five grand a week she was paying the men was starting to force their hunger to grow rapidly. After having a run-in with her top shotta Zero, he accepted the four hundred grand she offered to feed his entire crew the way he chose. It was much easier to hide out in the bounds of the island when a portion of her team gave up the security responsibilities for a few extra dollars. Now the two evil bitches were sitting around her crib drinking and eating as if they were in the breakfast lobby of the Marriott Hotel suites.

"So, big sister. What does it feel like to bond with me again since our last encounter? I mean, I love your hair. It's better than the last shitty hairdo you had before. Why don't you just be a good bitch, and call Laylah, and the rest of them here so I can handle this quickly?" Frost asked before biting into her glazed pastries.

"Because, bitch, unlike you, that's my blood sister. My true family. You're a wasted nut from my dad's ball sack. An accident. That's all you are." Mariah was breathing harshly from the beatings she had received over the past few hours. Her right eye had been swollen shut. Small cuts on her thighs and arms from Frost's hunting knife forced them to bleed slowly, and every time she delivered an answer that wasn't correct, she received a nasty backhand from one of the filthy Rastafarians standing next to her.

"Speaking of nut, let me wipe my mouth." Frost smiled, using a napkin to clean the white icing from the side of her lips. "I don't want it to look like a horny man jizzed on me. That actually doesn't sound like a bad idea for you, sister. I'm sure one of these horny, fat cock African men would love to abuse you before we leave, since we're here for nothing." She giggled.

"We're Jamaican, mon," one guard spoke.

"Shut the fuck up!" She pulled her gun, pointing it at his forehead. "I never asked you, and I'm quite sure I can tell the difference between races, motherfucker."

Placing her attention back on Mariah, Frost grinned. "By the time this bomb under your house blows, you'll be in heaven with God looking down on me while I'm slitting our father's throat. I'll leave the rest to you, Auntie." She cut her eyes over to Eva and snapped her fingers for the small army to follow.

"Fuck you!" Mariah spat under her breath.

Eva swallowed the last sip of her Long Island iced tea and set the glass on the table in front of her. Standing to her feet, she walked over to her great niece and smiled. "I know that you love him, darling, but your father has committed treason. He's part of a small bloodline that was supposed to be deleted so we, the Ramirezes, can grow and rise to our highest perfection. Don't let him bring you down like this. He's not even your biological sperm donor, for Christ sake." Eva shrugged, pulling a cigarette from her small hand purse.

"He's my dad all around in my eyes. You can beat the brain out of me and pluck my eyes from the sockets, and I would still be able to pick him out of two hundred men. He scarred you, the little Spanish side of people that truly has no relations to us. I understand, and I'm not sorry for none of you. I'll die knowing that I stood firm as a Grey so you don't have to waste your time talking anymore." Mariah spat the small glob of blood from her mouth.

She was sitting in a wooden chair, her hands and feet bound with zip ties. Her skin was sticky and hot, as if it were boiling from the hasty adrenaline rising in her body, and she couldn't help but to see her death approach as the time on the bomb clock ticked down slowly. Ten hours was all she had to think of a way out of the sticky situation, and Eva could feel the tension crawling from her skin.

Placing the cancer stick between her lips, Eva smiled. "Family could be your demise or your joy. I choose to let them be my peace. Unfortunately, I won't be at peace until Chance is resting in the belly of a shark, princess," she said, looking at the timer ticking on the small clock across from them. "You have a block of concentrated nitrogen and C4 bombs sitting in this room with you, and I can't be anywhere around when it sets off. I can't stop that time from moving, but since your dad is so special, I hope that he can get here to keep that bomb from popping your body apart like a hammer smashing a light-bulb. Then maybe you'll wish you were a Ramirez. I like your little security camera TVs you have down here. That'll give you something to watch before you pass on." She headed for the steps to leave.

Mariah knew that the tight plastic cutting into her skin would take time to break free from. The double wraps were squeezing harder than a python, and since her security had played the double cross, her only hope was to pray that some-one could make it down to her home before it ignited from the dangerous explosives that rested around her basement walls.

* * *

3:47 a.m.

Walking out of the airport doors, Justin and Courtney climbed inside of the Virgin Island taxi cab. The flight from Texas didn't take long. They had gotten the call from Reeses to come and assist Ghost with security for the family. There hadn't been a connection with the young queen since their last run in at the federal courthouse in Atlanta. It was the day she felt the two would cross her out for the government case the state was trying to pin against her. To Reeses' surprise, they held their loyalty and escaped the bounds of the law by fleeing off to build their own empire. After building up their money and connections with the corrupted side of the world, the drug corporation became a part of Justin's focus.

"Where will you be heading tonight?" the old islander asked with a smile from the front seat.

"We need to get to the boat dock so we can head for St. Croix. I need you to make it snappy too." Justin leaned forward, handing him a hundred dollar bill

"Of course." His tone became cheery upon seeing the American money.

Before he could pull off, the driver's door was snatched open and a pistol was placed down on his head with a pair of large arms snatching him out of the front seat.

"What the fuck?" Courtney jumped noticing the three armed guys who were now surrounding the taxi.

Justin tried to lock the back door, but it was quickly snatched open by a masked killer.

"Get the fuck out of the car before I blow out ya blot clot brain!" his Jamaican voice yelled while he pointed the assault rifle at him.

"Yo man, what the fuck? Just chill! We only tourists, man," he lied trying to keep his body in front of Courtney.

114

Kicking his feet at the attacker did nothing because the third man grabbed his legs, snatching him out of the backseat, forcing his head to connect with the pavement.

"Shittt!" He groaned in pain.

Courtney tried her best to scream and reach for the barrel of the gun he pointed down to Justin's head. Before she could stick her hand out of the car, the masked man squeezed the trigger, releasing two shots into his skull.

The flashes forced her to jump back and slide to the other side of the car door. The assassin that was still holding the old island man never noticed Suave creeping behind him smoother than a breeze of wind until the sharp blade slid across his throat. His arms released the elder and forced him to drop the pistol, and it was quickly picked up. By the time the other two were able to look back at their slain co-worker. Suave was aiming the weapon releasing every bullet that he could.

Boc! Boc! Boc! Boc! Boc!

The first three bullets found a home in the chest of the man who stood over Justin's dead body, and the next two jammed into the side of the man who was trying to snatch Courtney from the backseat.

"Fuck, mon!" he cried as the blood spilled from his rib cage, forcing him to fall down and use his feet to inch back away from the heartless murderer that was now standing over him. "Please don't kill me, mon! Me was paid to take care of the Grey family."

"I see. And that's the reason I'm taking care of you, pussy. Night-night," he whispered before placing another bullet between his eyes, watching his head snap back like a ketchup top.

A few citizens who moved around stood still and watched in horror, but it didn't cause Suave to freeze up. Moving quickly, he opened the back door and Courtney kicked her feet, trying to fight him off.

"Nooo, please don't do this!" she screamed, thinking that her life was about to end.

"Chill the fuck out and get the hell out of this car if you're not tryna die, 'cause I'm not about to wait around for any more of these bitches to come. Now!" Suave yelled.

Her chest heaved with fear, but she noticed that he wasn't filling her ass with any bullets, and that alone let her know that he was on her side. Climbing out of the backseat, she looked down at Justin and placed a hand over her mouth. "Justin!"

Suave grabbed her arm and began to run the opposite way. "Let's go, because his ass ain't coming back."

They made their way down the dark side where all the taxi cars were aligned. She ran directly by his side. "Who are you?"

"I should be asking you the same thing. I overheard you talking about coming here to help my brother while we were on the flight, and that's the only reason I pulled back to assist. How in the fuck y'all supposed to be killers and didn't see those dudes trail behind y'all after walking out of the damn airport?" Suave asked, nearly out of breath as he spotted a Toyota Camry sitting at the end of the block.

"I don't know. I didn't think we were being fucking followed. I'm only here because Justin wanted me to help out with protecting his family."

"Well obviously you don't know the type of help that this family needs. No one is ever safe at any time," Suave explained before breaking the glass window on the driver's side door. "Get in," he ordered.

Courtney quickly hopped in the passenger seat and he wasted no time snatching the box of wires from under the car's steering wheel. She watched as he flicked a few of them together, and before she could panic again, the engine came to life. Suave jacked the automatic into gear and slammed his foot on the gas pedal, smashing off into traffic.

Courtney sweated profusely, looking over at him. "Do you mind telling me what the fuck is going on?" Her hands were rubbing her head as if she couldn't believe what just transpired.

Suave kept his eyes on the road while shaking his head. "You got involved with the wrong family and didn't know that we got enemies on every block. I'll let him explain it to you when we get there. I don't do the question shit," he replied, making a sharp left turn.

All Courtney could do was sit back and ponder on what the fuck Reeses had just gotten her into.

Chris Green

Chapter 12
Downtown
Kingston, Jamaica

Sitting in his small office, General Cannon ended the phone call with his assistant. He was sure to place his three children on the first early morning boat to St. Croix. It was clear that he was about to prepare for an all-out war, and the safest place for them was on the big island that was beyond safeguarded. Regardless of the dangers within certain territories, he knew that Eva wouldn't have the heart to step foot on that rock, knowing that she would most likely be gunned down after reaching the shore. Out of fifteen years of being the enforcer of the police department of Jamaica, he'd never seen anyone with an army treading through St. Croix more loyal than the one Ms. Grey formed together. The killers down to the citizens praised her for the love she showed throughout the entire Croix. Her authority was well respected, and the money she would always disburse to the people is what caused them to dedicate their entire life to making sure that she would be recognized as the queen who changed the economy of their poverty-infested areas. Even with the top bosses who were able to make a name for themselves, she allowed them to see that family who moved as one, whether blood or not, they all could still eat together when it involved the Grey family.

"So, Mr. Cannon, how does it feel to spend your last few minutes wondering how you're gonna get away from a bullet and cheat death?" Torey said, easing smoothly through the door of his office.

His toxic tone sent a shivering chill up Cannon's spine. His pistol was sitting at the opposite end of his desk and too far to make a jump for it. When his eyes raised to look in Torey's eyes, his nose flared with a menacing grin as if he was daring the general to even budge an inch.

"What is the meaning of this? And if you have any idea of making it off this island without a bullet-riddled heart, you'll put the gun down. Let's talk like men."

Torey chuckled before placing a slug through his right shoulder. Pwet! His gun whistled lightly.

"Arghh! Blood clot, mon!" General Cannon howled in severe pain before biting down on his bottom lip.

"Now what in the fuck would possess you to talk shit at a nigga with the gun? I suggest you fix your attitude, sir, before you die now instead of when it's prescribed for ya, Ziggy bob."

"What is it that you want?"

Torey kept his eyes locked in on Cannon as he took a seat at the chair that sat directly in front of him. "The problem is your mouth, Cannon. From my understanding, you and my auntie had an agreement with the way she was gonna come handle business on the islands. You took 1.2 million and agreed that she would be free from all troubles with the law and from anyone running their mouth to the motherfuckers who we were here to eliminate. Correct?" Torey's eyes grew wide, waiting for him to state a lie.

"The only agreement me and Ms. Ramirez had was to come to the island for her business, and that I would not contact any higher authority as long as she kept her business discreet. Now I have nine innocent dead people in the morgue because of your family. Tell me, how does that business work?" Cannon was breathing harshly with a look of hate spilling from his face.

"Because, motherfucker, that's what happens when you're dealing with a family of murderers. Hits slip, and people die.

Do you tell Bob Marley that he can't smoke weed even though we know it's illegal in public? No, you don't, because we know this is the fucking ganja king, Cannon. So what you're saying is obsolete. We had a deal to keep the Greys unaware that our presence was here, pussy. That's what I'm speaking of. You snitched, bitch!" Torey hissed, tapping his silencer on the edge of the desk.

"Call it what you want, mon. I never gave up her whereabouts or her location. You don't think that it would have been easy to tell Ms. Grey that she was hiding out in Charlotte Amalie? They would have sent hundreds of Rastafarians to rip her guts out within the same fifteen minutes she received word. Your aunt is too loud and going against a family like the one you're toying with will leave all of you dead within a matter of days. It's only a matter of time," he spoke truthfully.

"Let me explain something to you, General Snitch. My family has waited decades to end this family affair. I've suffered since the age of one, wondering who I would murder once I was old enough to pull the trigger of a gun. From my understanding, it's actually a tradition, and that's something that neither you nor the law can interfere with. My aunt wants blood, and we are willing to go through you and anyone else to make it happen." Torey stood up to his feet. "So I'll offer you one last chance to save yourself. All we need is access to St. Croix. Give us the route to slide past his security so we can handle our family business, and you're free to go."

Cannon started to chuckle, and it eventually turned into a hysterical laugh, as if Torey had made the best joke of his life.

"Something I said funny to you?" Torey aimed his gun with a cynical expression.

"Yes, pussyhole young boy. Ms. Grey has shown me loyalty. More loyalty than my own people could ever offer me in a lifetime. I've blown through your aunt's lousy million dollars fifteen times plus since that family has touched the West Indie islands. You can cut my head from my body and send me on a first class trip through hell doused in gasoline, and I still wouldn't tell you how to get through St. Croix to harm them, regardless of how many traitors you all can get to side with you. If any of your people touch a small piece of that turf, you'll be dead before the shit turds fall down your pants leg. Now do what you came to do, faggot American boy," he hissed, still holding the bloody gunshot wound.

Torey smirked at the Jamaican's arrogance and shook his head. "You dumb banana boat-riding motherfuckers just don't like us city slickers do it. I'll be sure to tell Eva exactly what you wanted."

"You mean a dick up her filthy pussy."

"Nah. To have yo' shit chopped off and blazed up like those nasty-ass beef patties ya sister serves, bitch!" he spat before crashing the butt of his gun across Cannon's temple, knocking him unconscious. He placed him in a pair of cuffs. He dragged his body out of the office, past the three dead officers on the floor.

Chapter 13
St. Thomas, 8:15 a.m.

Ghost, Stone, and Shadow stepped out of the rented SUV at the bottom of Mariah's home. The long trail leading up to her mini mansion was definitely made for security purposes because a car wasn't sliding through the thin pathway unless it was able to transform into a human.

"Who murdered the fucking driveway?" Shadow laughed.

"I was just about to ask the same shit. This bitch look like it was made for a snake parade trail," Ghost said, leading the way up the funny slanted hill. "Where in the fuck is all these so-called bodyguards she supposed to have watching this bitch? If we made it to the bottom of her shit with no guns letting loose, something's wrong."

The natural feeling in his gut said that there was a problem, especially after noticing that Mariah hadn't been taking his phone call since last night. The one thing he knew about his oldest was her firmness on staying honest and never making an excuse for not standing on whatever she agreed to. Since he'd woken from his slumber with Tiffany and Erica this morning. He realized that she still had yet to make it across the water to St. Croix, and that wasn't the understanding before their video call ended last night.

"Yo Shadow, when have you ever known Mariah to pass down being around me?" Ghost asked to see if he could get the same reaction from him.

"Maybe when you were taking a crap on the toilet. Besides that, she would stay stuck to ya like glue, dawg. Why you ask?"

"Because I haven't seen my child in over ten years, and she literally went the entire night without rushing over to be around me," Ghost said, removing the pistol from his shoulder holster.

The bright sky that had been simmering most of the morning was starting to form a few dark clouds, and the statement his friend just made caused a slight grumble in his stomach. "Do you think something's wrong, bro?"

"You tell me. We been walking up this long-ass trail for a whole minute, and haven't seen one nigga who supposed to be protecting my daughter yet." Ghost paused in his tracks, looking back at him and Stone.

He could tell that both of them felt the same way from how their eyes locked, and they removed their weapons. Ghost never allowed his feelings to lead him wrong, and once his instincts smelt fuckery, more than likely, that's what it was.

* * *

Mariah could feel the second thermoplastic on her right arm slowly coming loose as she grinded her wrist back and forth on the wooden chair, allowing the friction to split it apart slowly. Her eyes just looked at the timer, which read four minutes, and she was sweating profusely trying to break free from the restraints. The next thing her eyes spotted on the security TV screens caused her heart to beat like a car speaker. "Daddy," she whispered, spotting Ghost walking with Shadow and Stone up the long walk trail of her home. She jolted her eyes back to the timer that was now ticking at under three minutes. She started to move her wrist faster, scraping it against the thick wooden arm. "Pleaseee break! Break!" she yelled, feeling the small trail of blood leaking off the bottom of her arm from the small knife wounds that reopened. Her mind was starting to go in a panic, and just when it seemed like all hope could be lost, her first wrist broke free from the death gripping restraint. "Yes!" she mumbled, going straight to the second arm, using her teeth and hand strength.

She could see her father nearly reaching the top of the hill where the gate of the home rested, and if he stepped foot in her home without a warning of the bomb that was counting down, not only would she lose, but it would take out half of her family in the same motion. Once the two restraints from her arms were off, she trembled, moving down to her feet. The ticker from the bomb read one minute and forty-seven seconds, and she refused to let it all end before connecting back with her father.

"I'm not gonna die like this." She snatched wildly at the plastic, breaking off a nail. The blood that oozed from her fingertips didn't faze her with everyone's life being at stake. Mariah's lips fidgeted hard, and using her last bit of strength, the zip ties popped loose, allowing her to break free.

"Dadddyyyy, don't come in!" she screamed at the top of her lungs as if he could hear her through the thick walls. Scrambling to her feet, she sped up the basement steps.

Chris Green

Chapter 14

After trailing up the long walkway, the guys finally made it to the top of her residence. Ghost could see the large gate that sat at a small distance, but the next thing his eyes spotted caused him to hit Shadow's shoulder. A dead bodyguard could be seen lying face down on the ground, and judging from the pile of dark blood that ran from underneath his body, he damn sure wasn't sunbathing. Raising their guns, they all began to look around the perimeter, knowing that Eva's treacherous ass had definitely made an appearance. Ghost was the first one that stepped his foot through the threshold of the large gate, as Shadow and Stone followed. That was the last movement the guys were able to make before what happened next.

Ghost's eyes landed on Mariah's front door as it was snatched open.

"Daddy, get backkk!" she screamed at the top of her lungs.

"Mariah?" His heart dropped as he ran towards her.

The loud explosion that erupted afterwards vaporized her entire body and the house before they could even get within a hundred feet of each other's reach. The impact alone caused Ghost, Shadow, and Stone to get pushed back through the steel gate, nearly sending them twenty feet away. The house was sent into a million pieces through the air.

Struggling to raise his body off the ground, Ghost looked at what used to be his daughter's home and started to scream. "Mariahhhh!" He struggled to jump back to his feet and head for the burning building.

Shadow quickly hopped up and grabbed a hold of him. "Ghost, stop. You can't go in there, dawg. She's gone, bro."

"Get the fuck off me, man! That's my daughter in there!" he yelled, thinking that she was still alive somewhere behind the large flames.

All Shadow could do was hold his partner back until he crashed to the ground in pain. Tears streamed from his eyes as the thick cloud of smoke floated gently into the air.

Stone struggled to rise from the ground and grabbed a hold of his gun that was a few feet away from him. "I don't think we should prolong and sit right here, Ghost. I know that this is a tragic moment right now, but we might be sitting ducks for Eva if she's anywhere near here."

"He's right, bro, we have to go." Shadow held his shoulder, trying to console him as he wept for the soul of his oldest child.

All he could think about was letting the young soldier Tre down with raising his biological princess as his own. He vowed to protect her by any means, and that promise was broken. Eva was behind the horrendous act, and he felt it coming from a mile away.

"Call Erica and Tiffany to let them know. We have to make sure they're on point 'cause if this bitch got close to Mariah like this, there's no telling if she snooping around St. Croix," he replied before wiping the tears from his face.

Shadow helped him up to his feet and they all began to trail back down to the parked Tahoe SUV that rested at the bottom of her trail path. It took five minutes to make it back to where they started, and they could still smell the burning gases lingering in the air. The sound of fire trucks and an ambulance could be heard wailing at a distance. Ghost looked back one last time and pictured Mariah's sweet face before getting in the passenger seat.

Stone was dialing Reeses' number on his cell phone before climbing in the back, and Shadow made his way around to the driver's side and got in, starting the ignition. He let the tires screech through the dry dust as they headed back for the boat dock.

"Shadow?" Ghost mumbled with his head hanging low in grief.

"Wassup, folk?"

"I don't know if I can keep my good spirit anymore, bro. Put more soldiers on the lurk for those bitches, and let them know I'll give three million to whoever can bring them alive. Until then, we moving out every night, killing everything that looks like a traitor. I want every Jamaican head that was supposed to be protecting my daughter." His eyes glared with a look of pain.

"I got you, dawg. That's my word."

Shadow placed his attention back on the road. He knew one thing for sure. The newly reformed Ghost had quickly faded away, and the pandemonium he was about to release was sure to shake the water underneath the islands.

Chris Green

Chapter 15
The Grey mansion

Tiffany couldn't do anything but cry along with Laylah as they sat in the living room of their large estate. The news that Reeses just delivered shattered her young heart to pieces and left everyone else distraught. Courtney and Suave arrived earlier that morning, and in just the first few hours they were struck hard by the loss of Ghost's oldest child. The small bond Suave shared with his niece when she was just a toddler was the last memory that he could actually say he held on to. The ruthless disrespect from Eva had him quiet and craving to detach her head himself. Out of respect for Erica and Tiffany telling him to remain calm, he held his composure until Ghost arrived back at the crib.

It wasn't even thirty minutes after receiving the information from Stone, and Erica had already placed a million dollar bounty on Mariah's head security Zero. He was the lead enforcer, and supposedly the most loyal protector to watch over her. It didn't take long for a response, because after her hit was made, he was being dragged through the front door of her home brutally beaten in a pair of cuffs. The side of his face was swollen and bleeding profusely, half of his dreads were missing, and a large bullet hole was in the center of his right kneecap.

The salty tears were still running down Erica's face as she stood with her pistol in hand. Zero had enough energy to reach out and touch her red bottom heels, smearing a small line of blood across them. Raising her right leg, she screamed, stomping down on his shit forcefully.

"Whyyyy?"

His mouth was wide open as he gasped with horrible pain, but no sound could escape his windpipe.

"Where did you find him?" She looked in the eyes of her trusted bodyguard Sleeper.

"The team out in John's caught him clearing his house out to bail from the islands. His kids and wife were murdered on the spot, and there was over a half million dollars in the trunk of his car. Your word is final, boss lady, and me have no problem severing him into dog food right now." Sleeper mugged the traitor with his M-16 assault rifle pointing down at his skull.

"No. My husband will want the honors of that. Anyone who was assigned to Mariah's station… I want all of them murdered, whether they were involved or not. Whoever was in his crew, execute them in front of the entire island.

"Yes ma'am."

"Chain him up to the water pipe down in the basement, and I'll be sure to have your money accounted for by morning," Erica ordered with authority.

Sleeper nodded his head as he and another guard started to drag Zero down to his new graveyard.

"I say we head out and find this bitch on our own. Since she's lookin' for us, we can bring the bullshit straight to wherever this hoe is at. She killed our daughter, Erica. How much longer can we sit here and wait?" Tiffany voiced with anger in her tone.

"You don't think I know that, Tiff? I'm hurt just like you, baby, but you know that Ghost is gonna want to move a certain way with this now. They've shed the blood of our child, and I won't rest until we have eliminated everybody that's standing with her."

"I don't care who's involved. I want in. My cousin's death will not be in vain, and letting go of some shit like this will not be accepted." Reeses stomped out of the living room.

Before Erica could respond, the sound of a distant helicopter could be heard hovering in the air. Hearing Frost's voice boom through a megaphone, Erica, Tiffany, and Laylah rushed out to the backyard, looking up at the aircraft floating gently in the air above the large ocean of water. Her voice grew louder.

"Attention, world. General Cannon of the Jamaican police force has decided to make a decision that would be extremely hazardous and tragic for his life. Today was the day he vowed to not give up the secrets of the Grey family's location and security forces. This idiot was willing to risk his life for a bunch of cocksucking nobodies who now have to watch him die in vain!" she screamed loudly as the giant chopper floated closer to the island.

Frost's eyes looked down at the large area of land, praying that her distant relatives were somewhere on the giant rock watching the live show, because the catastrophes would never stop until they all collided harder than a hurricane and tsunami. General Cannon sat bound at the edge of the helicopter's rail with a thick rope secured around his neck.

"This man was faithful for a poor cause, and now it is time for him to receive the wish he asked for. Any last words, General Cannon?" She placed the megaphone up to his mouth as if he really wanted to shout out thank you's to all of his criminal fans. His eyes stared at her with no fear, and instead of speaking, he smiled with a devilish grin. His vision roamed over St. Croix. He spotted the Grey's family mansion and hoped that his children would remain safe under the protection of Erica's warm love.

"Well, I guess that's a no, people." Frost sat down the megaphone and grabbed the can of gasoline, pouring a small amount over his head, and the rope. She kicked him from the chopper, causing his neck to snap like a tree twig. As his loose body dangled, she lit the rope, watching as the flame trailed down to him within seconds. His body ignited quickly, turning him into a ball of fire.

Erica and Tiffany looked on in amazement, knowing that Frost had literally lost her fucking mental with the stunt. General Cannon was a valuable asset to them, and they were proving with every treacherous step that they wanted war. Stepping on St. Croix was nearly impossible, so forcing them off was the next in line if there was no other way to make them see the picture vividly.

The rope holding General Cannon's body snapped, forcing it to fall down into the water beneath the helicopter as Frost laughed wickedly through the megaphone. The man steering the aircraft turned the opposite way, speeding off, letting her dreadful giggle drift off with the wind.

Tiffany placed a hand over her mouth, watching the sickening murder take place. Erica turned back around to head back in the home, and her eyes looked up at Cannon's three boys staring out of the guest bedroom window. Judging from the tears streaming down their faces, they saw the tragic event of their father's demise.

"These people have gotten out of hand. If Chance doesn't push the right way after tonight, we're gonna have to take matters into our own hands. I've sent Sleeper to clean house on anyone who's sliding on their stomachs, and that'll leave room for us to block off all the private docks to box these bitches in," Erica stated with assurance.

"So what do you want me to do?" Tiffany asked, ready to bust her guns for the family.

"Worry about comforting him tonight so he doesn't have to grieve so hard about Mariah. Tomorrow I'm calling an all-out manhunt for the both of them, and we're moving out ourselves this time. I refuse to let a totally different bloodline spill the lives of loved ones and move around like the Greys are powerless in our own territory," she replied before walking back into the house.

Laylah stood beside her with a stale look. Her hands were tucked inside her Valentino jeans, and Tiffany knew what she was waiting for. She didn't like to bring the dark side out of her, but she was the best at what was so badly needed: bringing peace.

"Laylah, Mommy needs you to go take a shower and clear your mind. Erica is gonna need your help tomorrow, and I'm giving you permission to end this. We can't lose your father again, baby." Tiffany looked into her matching green eyes with

"Yes, Mama," she answered with a cold stare before leaving her in the backyard.

Tiffany exhaled deeply, glancing down at her sky blue Dolce and Gabbana dress and the white slide-on Louis Vuitton slippers on her feet. Years of retirement were finally about to be replaced with something that she promised to leave put up forever. It was all for the sake of family, and if that meant she had to place it all on the line in order to see them stay together, then it was damn sure about to be written in stone.

Chris Green

Chapter 16

The bright sky that was recently shining clearly was replaced with a gloomy dark hue and strong gusts of wind. The house was completely silent until Ghost, Shadow, and Stone crossed the threshold. Tiffany was the first to jump to her feet and embrace him in a tight hug. "Are you okay?"

He kissed her and nodded with a scarred expression. "I need y'all to hear something." His cell phone was in his hand as he walked closer to Erica while she sat with Laylah on the white leather couch.

He pressed the number five on his dial pad and Eva's voice started to talk clearly through the speaker.

"Hello, Chance. It seems that after all these long years I've finally gotten to see you have someone so precious and dear to you taken away. At first I wanted to be kind and spare the lives of the ones who never caused harm for me, but I realized that the only things that pierce through your tough skin are when you lose one of your own. I felt the same way losing my three sons that you took away from me. Pain is something that you've had yet to feel, Chance. So I'll make you a deal. Your life for the rest of the Grey family to live free without any more worries. Your poor little seed won't rest until you're six feet under, so be considerate. You have six hours to answer back or the bloody drama shall continue," Eva explained before Frost started to yell through the line.

"Yeah, what she said! The drama will fucking continue, and I'm killing——" was all she got to shout before the voicemail ended

Tiffany rubbed a hand through her hair in aggravation. "These bitches have some real nerve. They're playing this duck-duck-goose game as if we aren't ready to die about ours!"

"I know, Tiff, but I've made enough bad decisions with underestimating these tricks. I don't want to slip and lose anyone else. I'll just sacrifice myself and handle the business on my own," Ghost suggested.

"You sound crazy, as if I didn't spend sixteen years behind the wall to hear you talk like this. If you at war, we all are," Suave said with a menacing tone.

"He's right, Chance, so you might as well wipe that out of your mind." Erica raised his head to look in his eyes. "Mariah's bodyguard is down in the basement, and if anybody knows something, it has to be him."

"What?" Ghost gave her a look as if he might have heard wrong.

Nodding at him to give assurance that he wasn't deaf, she placed her pistol into his palm. Ghost declined by giving it back and moved over to Shadow.

"Let me see the knife." He held out his hand.

He knew that his brother's mind wasn't right after losing another child, and denying him was definitely out of the equation. Walking over to his leather jacket, Shadow removed his stainless samurai sword and placed it in his hand.

Ghost didn't hesitate to head straight for the bottom floor of the mansion. He strolled down the long corridor until he reached a dark mahogany door. He stepped through it and headed down the steps two at a time. Reaching the ground floor, his eyes landed on Zero dangling from the ceiling. His head was dropped down into his chest, and the blood from his wounds was forming a puddle underneath him.

Walking over to him, Ghost grabbed his face forcefully. His eyes were filled with a deadly aura as he spoke. "She was only nineteen, motherfucka! You crossed my baby girl out for a check that I could've given you fifty times over. I need to know where that bitch Eva is laying low. Then I may think about killing you with a bullet to make it quick."

Zero's incoherent murmuring started to subside when Ghost slammed a fist into his right eye. The punch even caused Erica to flinch as she stood in the middle of the staircase watching from a distance.

"Blood clot, mon! Me only did what the lady forced upon me family. She tried to kill my gal and young one, bad man. Me swear on my life. No one stood for the young Grey gal like me boss man!" he cried. The punch instantly closed his eye shut and it felt as if he could feel a pulse quaking through it with every second that passed.

"No one can make a killer do anything, bitch-ass nigga!" Ghost barked. "You gave in because you were weak, and that cost the life of my baby. Where is she?"

"I was never aware of where the bright lady lay her head, mon. Respect runs in me bones for ya, but I still not an informer. Just kill as a killer should." He glared into Ghost's eyes, knowing that death was awaiting him regardless of what he said.

"Just remember I offered you to go quick."

Ghost grabbed the back of his head with a psychotic look. He pushed the blade into his throat slowly. His dark, thick blood started to ooze down his shirt, turning it cardinal red. His body shook horribly as Ghost slid the blade down, dividing his neck like an overcooked hot link. Pulling it out forcefully, he jammed it down into his chest and severed him down to the stomach.

Erica covered her mouth and quickly headed back up the steps, being sure not to be seen. The devastating sight of his torture was too much, and just judging from what her eyes viewed, she knew that the same man who left ten years ago was surely still living with them.

Digging his hand inside of Zero's chest, Ghost snatched out his heart and tossed it on the tile floor. "That's what happens when you're not a killer wholeheartedly, nigga." He grimaced before hawking a glob of spit in his face.

Removing his T-shirt, Ghost wiped the blood from his hands and Shadow's sword. He took a minute to calm himself before making any sudden moves. Walking back up to the top floor, he entered the living room, handing the weapon back to his partner in crime.

"Zero didn't wanna cooperate, so we're gonna stick to the plan. Since you all won't allow me to die for the cause, we need more help, because just us ain't gonna cut it."

Erica knew that he was snapping back to his old ways when their eyes locked. "You didn't have to sit on the steps and watch. She was your daughter also, and you had just as much rights as me, Queen. We need to contact Cannon and let him know that we may need some reinforcements."

"That's not gonna work, baby," Tiffany chimed in, remembering the fucked-up execution from earlier.

"What do you mean?"

"Frost got rid of him earlier. She flew him over the island from a rope around his neck while he was burning alive. This shit has passed another level already. We're gonna need more than some extra help. We need an army," she spoke truthfully.

Erica moved over to Ghost, whispering in his ear. Everybody knew that there were no such things as secrets, but the expression he gave said that a few things had to be kept personal for safety purposes.

"Come upstairs with me." He grabbed her hand. "Tiffany, call Sleeper and let him know that we need as many recruits as we can. I'm willing to spend every coin I got to see every shooter on these islands behind us."

"I'm on it," she said before he disappeared upstairs.

140

Walking up to the second level of their home, Ghost moved towards the guest room that sat next to Laylah's and opened the door. The three young Jamaican boys that sat on the bed eyed him with curiosity, wondering what his presence was for. The oldest of the three stood to his feet, ready to protect his twin brothers by any means necessary. Erica stood behind Ghost, knowing the children were hurting deeper than pain could explain after watching their father's death this morning from a window.

Ghost got on one knee and held out a hand to the young soldier. His wavy hair and green eyes didn't give him the image of an island boy, nor did his bright red skin. Ghost could tell that he was nervous, but General Cannon's loyalty to the family was so powerful that his children wouldn't want for anything as long as he walked the earth's ground.

"Wassup, li'l man? I'm Ghost. What's ya name?"

"Blaze," he spoke with a thick accent, verifying that he was definitely born in Jamaica.

"Blaze, I know this is a hard time for you and your little brothers right now, but I just wanna let you know that we're all family here. Your dad was close to us, which makes you all close also. You all will never want for nothing, and I promise that you'll be safe here if you're willing to accept my offer."

"I not know who to trust anymore, Ghost." His arms were folded looking back at the twins to see if they agreed.

They jumped off the bed and both ran over to Ghost, hugging him around the neck.

Embracing the young ones, Ghost looked at Blaze with a smile. "Does that mean we good?"

"Yes sir. That's Fyah, and that's Maxus."

Ghost nodded with approval. "Let me ask you something, Blaze."

"Yes sir?"

"Does your father have a home in Jamaica where he keeps his things to protect you guys?"

"If you mean guns, I can take you to his storage."

Ghost smiled with a shrug before looking up at Erica.

Chapter 17
2:36 a.m.

After sending Shadow and Stone on the mission to Jamaica with Cannon's oldest son earlier, Ghost found himself sitting in the room, thinking of memories of Mariah when she was just a small baby. Her laugh, her stubbornness to always be up under him… She was the perfect piece to the family, the baby that carved her way in as a Grey. Even thoughts of Bernard struck him.

After falling asleep for what he thought was just a few hours, he found himself being woken up from Erica's hand caressing down his chest. The sound of Dreezy's song "Close to You" was playing softly through their Panasonic surround sound system. The light from the bathroom shone brightly on him as Tiffany opened it and posted in the doorway. Her luscious red thighs and ass were eating her pink Gucci thong alive. Her juicy breasts were mounted in the matching bra like a set of coconuts from a palm tree. He couldn't help but to lick his lips eagerly as she dropped her long black hair out of the ponytail it was wrapped in.

Erica's hand was sliding down under the covers to his piece, pulling it gently from his boxers, as Tiffany made her way over to the bed, climbing inside. Ghost tried to sit up and was pushed back down.

"Don't move, daddy. Just let us please you tonight." Erica's seductive voice was low, demanding his cooperation.

Doing as he was told, he instantly became aroused as they both sat on the bed, stripping before him. Their breasts, hips, and backsides were so captivating and mouthwatering that he could feel the tantalizing orgasm rising in his shaft.

Hiking their asses in the air, they both took turns downing him slowly. Lick for lick, they would share him equally like two children feasting off one Push Pop. Spitting on his dick, Erica massaged it, forcing his man to stand at a crooked angle.

"Damn, ma," he grunted, watching Tiffany apply the same treatment.

The soft music was enticing their energy and naughty behavior, especially when they started to kiss passionately on the head and his stomach.

Erica did the first honors with mounting him cowgirl style to let him get a full view of her juicy apple sliding down easily on the monster. The first stroke caused her to arch it higher, rising to the top.

"Sss, damn, baby," she whined, pouting out her lips like a bad schoolgirl. After catching the groove of his masterpiece, she rocked her hips, letting it bounce recklessly. His hands moved to her hips down to her ass. He couldn't help but to slap a firm hand down on it to see that thing jiggle everywhere.

Tiffany kissed Erica's breast while twirling her love button in a circular motion. Ghost bit his bottom lip, watching her sweet white passion caking up around the base of his dick. It was heaven. The sticky sounds alone made her slow down to look back at her man's face. His eyes were low, and judging from the way his lips curled, he was enjoying that shit. Squatting up, she then dropped that ass down like a bad habit, forcing his head to tilt. Her ass clapped loudly against his pelvis, and taking control was no longer about to be passed. Locking on to her waist, he pounded forcefully, and her kitty spoke with delight.

"Fuckkk!" she panted, holding on to one of his arms as her juices started to spill down on his stomach. His nine inches were digging so deep that her orgasm forced her to slide off the hypnotizing magic stick.

Tiffany wasted no time cleaning up her spill with a few licks and slurps to Ghost's manhood. "Sss…yummy." Her green eyes sparkled with explicitness.

His hand moved quickly to Erica's warm spot as she laid gently on the side of him. Her wet lips soaked his fingers as he moved them up and down.

Climbing on top for her turn, Tiffany never took her eyes from his. Her hands would rub up and down his chest as she started to grind on his pole nastily.

Her ass was so big that he couldn't help but grab a handful while her breasts bounced freely. It was beautiful. The Queens of his world were pleasing him greatly, and nothing felt better than watching them share their love on one another.

Ghost spread her ass, allowing his dick to plunge in the pussy. Fuck making love. He was trying to make another family all in one night. His adrenaline was on Energizer Bunny, and fucking around with the ass, he would die from being drained out by morning.

Lifting Tiffany up, he rolled over on top of her and lifted her thick red thighs. That pretty heart-shaped pussy stuck out at him like a sore thumb, and he wasted no time diving in.

"That's right, daddy. Get yo' pussy." She took his punishment like a good freak should.

"Who it belong to?" he teased with a long stroke, feeling her gushy walls squeeze around his shit.

"You, baby. It's yours. I swear it is." Tiffany's eyes began to roll as she felt a massive nut approaching.

Ghost couldn't help but to handle that business, knowing moments like the one he was experiencing rarely sparked when there was so much drama revolving around them. After a full hour of tasting their sweet splits and filling them both with equal strokes of passion, they both sat on their knees, enjoying his vanilla rain shower.

Cuddling deeply into the Giorgio Armani bedspreads, he held on to them both with his eyes closed. Erica kissed his cheek as Tiffany's head rested on his chest. Looking into her dark brown eyes, she gave him another peck.

"I just wanna let you know that we move as one, Chance. You're not leaving here anymore by yourself, and if we go out, we'll just have to go out as one. That's what family is for, daddy," Erica spoke with sincerity.

"I know, baby. Try and get you some sleep, Queen." He rubbed a finger down her cheek delicately.

Smiling, she cuddled under his right side, and he knew that she was his spitting image. Her anger had gotten worse, but her dedication to pleasing him and Tiffany was the reason his love ran so deep. The fate of his family was on the line, and he was willing to perish before allowing them to be harmed again. That was a vow he placed on his children's lives.

Chapter 18
St Thomas; Charlotte Amalie
The next day, 7:48 p.m.

Coco sat in the room debating on whether or not to make the call she so badly wanted to. The deeply grievous news about Mariah's death was the last line that her daughter and slime associate Eva crossed. It was true that she gave them the permission to hunt Ghost down for the critical assassination attempt on her, but taking the life of his other children was against everything they agreed upon. The guilt of the young girl's death was eating at her conscience like maggots on pork in the sun, and that was a family legacy that she refused to be a part of.

Instead of wasting any more time, she dialed the number into her HTC touchscreen phone. Her eyes closed after the first ring sounded in her ear. Once his voice finally ran through the line, she stumbled to reply.

"Who is this?" His tone alone sent a menacing chill through her flesh and bones.

"It's me, Ghost, and before you tell me the thoughts on your mind and what you're gonna do, just please hear me out. Since the last time I saw you so long ago, I prayed for your demise. I dreamed of you day and night, wondering how you slept knowing that you nearly ended my life for a small mistake. I never saw myself ending up on your bad side, nor did I ever feel that you would be the one who came so close to doing the same to the ones I grew to love as my own. Regardless of how much I wanted to see you gone, I never intended on seeing anything happen to your precious seeds. I wouldn't stoop so low with my treachery because the vendetta was between me, you, and the woman in your life that I chose to disrespect - a decision that I regret every day when I look in the mirror and see my condition. I didn't have enough guts to call you, but the shit that was pulled on your innocent children was something I just couldn't accept. Charlotte Amalie is where you will end it all if you move quick enough. I'm sorry," Coco spoke truly from the heart, wiping away her small trail of tears.

A small moment of silence filled the air before he finally replied. "Much appreciated, Coco, and I'll think about that once I remove your life for good this time," he said before ending the call.

Coco's heart skipped a beat from the calm threat he delivered, and it was damn sure that he was gonna make good on his mission to end her life.

Quickly deleting the information from her call log, she pondered on how to get the hell away from the distant island town before her child's father made his approach. The life she lived after her tragedy was perfect. She couldn't help but to look around the luxurious mansion at the major accomplishments that had been gained since the day her life was nearly taken. The large living room. Clean lines drew the eye to the pergola entry, where a vibrant teal front door was flanked by a nine foot wall of glass. Black slate floors mixed with red wood panels were laced in the large family room. There was a stylish kitchen and a dining area with a wet bar. The house was furnished with exquisite furnishings, and a dual-sided stone fireplace ran from the floor to the ceiling. There was no limit to what their pockets could afford, and still Coco felt like she was out of place.

Frost strolled smoothly around the corner of the dining room with a mischievous grin on her evil face while she was in deep thought. "Hey Mama, who were you just talking to?"

Coco could feel the sneakiness crawling off her daughter's skin and wondered if she truly heard anything that was just said. Instead of folding, she stood firm. "Myself, darling. I've been losing focus, and a little self-motivation was needed," she lied.

"Mm-hmm. You've been fine. Why has it changed all of a sudden?"

"Because things change, Frost. Why are you questioning me? I'm your mother?" she answered with a slight tone of agitation.

"Because you're a fucking rat!" She pulled her gun, aiming directly for Coco's head.

Staring down the huge barrel forced her heart to thump awkwardly offbeat as if it was playing a hip hop track. "Frost, I don't know what the hell has gotten into you over these past few weeks, but I need you to calm down before you end up doing something reckless, honey," she begged with her chest heaving harder than a track runner.

Eva strolled through the door, catching the action first hand, and slowly walked into the mix. "Have you lost your mind, little girl? Put that fucking gun down now and explain what the meaning of this is!"

Frost pointed a stern finger towards her mother as if Eva couldn't see her sitting on the couch. "I think she's working with somebody. I heard her talking on the phone to someone about us. Check her phone!"

"Frost, are you high, or is this a joke?" Eva folded her arms with a straight face. "She's your mother and has stood by you through whatever."

"That's your fucking opinion. Check her phone." She kept her eyes locked in on Coco.

Eva moved over to Coco, picking up the touchscreen from beside her. Pressing the dial pad, she scrolled through the call log, reviewing the last few numbers that were dialed. After checking thoroughly, she even tapped the message box to make sure her niece wasn't exaggerating. With a pissed expression, she tossed it to Frost, watching her catch it.

"Now that I see you've literally lost your damn mind, I'll remember to double check things behind your ass before any more decisions can be made. Lower the damn gun."

Frost's angry face faded. She felt that she may have gone slightly overboard. Dropping her arm down, she looked back, and forth between both of them. "I may have heard wrong."

"You think?" Coco shouted with tears in her eyes. "You're nothing I expected you to be. After all these years of searching for this man, I think that it's really messed your head up. You didn't keep your mind on the main mission, and that's something I will never respect, whether you're my child or not. You murdered that innocent girl Mariah when you agreed to keep the bloodshed focused on two people - the ones who caused all of the drama!" she yelled.

Frost squinted her eyes before slowly raising her head to look in Coco's eyes. "I never told you I killed Mariah. Who did you hear that from?" She caught Coco totally off guard with the question.

Eva paused, gazing at Coco after the words escaped her niece's lips.

"I overheard you speaking to a guard. You promised that this wasn't going to happen, Frost. You've placed us under deep water with this," she spoke nervously.

"Eavesdropping instead of speaking on it at the time makes it a secret - a secret to give away, so the pressure could be released off of you. But the question is, for *who*?"

Eva had to pause and gaze at her once she realized what escaped her lips.

The moment Coco stuttered, Frost raised her gun, squeezing the trigger. The slug ripped through the center of Coco's forehead, forcing her eyes to roll off to the dark side, causing

Eva to jump. The large bloodstain covering the couch dripped smoothly down to the pillows as her body tilted over.

"Frost! What in the fuck is wrong with you?" Eva's lips trembled, ready to drop tears for the woman she considered to be a daughter.

Ignoring her sympathetic statement, Frost placed the gun back in her shoulder holster. Taking the thin quilt that was laying on the living room's mantel piece, she tossed it over Coco's body and turned her attention back to Eva. "You're the same one who taught me the principles of family, and that treason was a rule that we were to never cross. I'm here to end what we created, and our protection is a must if we want to make it back home safely. If anyone decides to come in between that, family or associates, they die. Simple. Hopefully you haven't gone weak on me and started to respect the same things that we stand against?" Frost asked with a raised eyebrow.

Eva shook her head, knowing that the little devil in front of her was possessed with more than a demonic spirit. But still and all, the words that she spoke were true. Cracking a smile, she dug in her cleavage, pulling out a Newport cigarette. After sparking it with the lighter from her glass and steel-framed coffee table, Eva exhaled. "I was only weak for you and Coco, but I guess that just leaves you now. Have the guards dispose of her, and get ready to discuss the plans with your cousin Torey and the new crew members."

"Now that sounds like my auntie." Frost smiled wickedly, pinching her cheek before walking off.

Chris Green

Chapter 19
The Grey mansion

Ghost stood in the middle of his living room fully dressed for the war that was about to occur. His black Kevlar bulletproof vest was strapped on tight. He was carrying his pearl-handled Glock 40 and a Ruger nine millimeter on his hip holsters. Shadow, Suave, Erica, Tiffany, and Stone stood to the side, waiting until he ended the phone call with Sleeper. Laylah was fully dressed with her gear, along with Reeses, and half of their front parking lot was filled with thirty-seven sick Jamaican shootas ready to kill for fun. After getting the miracle call from Coco explaining to him the whereabouts of Eva and Frost, Ghost alerted every island to cut off all exits. Tonight was the night that they would pay with their own souls for the foul play they committed, even if it meant that he had to drown in the same pit with them.

After Sleeper confirmed that he had another twenty-two men heavily armed and waiting for them with the transportation trucks at the boat dock of St Thomas, Ghost ended the call and turned to his family.

"It's time. We're gonna flush this shit out and make it back home as a team. The mansion is out in a secluded wooded area inside of Charlotte Amalie. We're gonna break up into four groups, and no matter what happens, you're not allowed to break apart for shit. That's why we have our group of shooters running in first to eliminate whatever they view in sight. We're the cleanup crew to ensure these bitches die where they stand. Me, Erica, Shadow, and Sleeper will be in a group. Tiffany, Laylah, Suave, and Stone will be in the second. Reeses and Courtney will hold down the vehicles out front with an eight man crew to ensure that we're ready to leave after this is settled. I know that we've lost a lot in these past few years, but tonight we feast and show these mutherfuckers why the Grey family remains unstoppable," he said, looking around at them all and pulling the latch on his P90 semi-automatic. "Now let's end this shit!"

As the family spilled out into the front driveway of their home, Ghost looked around at all the men. "Let's ride out. We breaking off in four groups after we leave the boat dock in St. Thomas. We don't show any mercy, so be prepared to bust yo' gun the same way you was quick to take the money I hired you with." Ghost looked at Sleeper's young killer, who was in charge of the foreigners.

He replied with a finger sliding across his throat, whistling twice. The small army moved quicker than mice loading up in the Infiniti and GMC trucks.

Ghost climbed in the whip, letting Shadow take the driver's seat. Erica took the back and started to load her two 45 Kimber automatic pistols. Seven vehicles pulled out from his driveway, leaving ten men behind to secure the property. The gloves were finally about to be snatched off, and Ghost was damn sure gonna be the first to make a move.

***

Charlotte Amalie
One hour later

Strolling around the large meeting room on the second floor, Frost explained to Torey and the newly recruited Trenchtown Jamaican killers on their team how shit was gonna play out for the invasion in St. Croix. Knowing that it was a dangerous stunt, she was willing to sacrifice a few of the idiots to get her hand on the grand prize: Ghost.

"Now that we've got things mapped out with how many men will proceed through the beach side of their residence… I'll assist the ones who crush the docks, and Torey will lead the crew through the back projects of Croix and approach from the blindside."

"That all sounds good and all, but we have twenty men sitting in this room with us, and over twenty downstairs in your basement waiting for demands. If it's that easy, why don't we just make our way to St. Croix tonight and eat on that shit?"

The moment his words spilled from his lips, God placed his wishes on the front doorstep of their hideout. The power in the house blanked out, leaving them moving friskily in the dark.

"What the fuck?" Torey mumbled, pulling out his burner. "Did y'all pay the bills in the bitch?"

The guards in the room began to clutch on their weapons, but Frost stood still listening for anything out of the ordinary. After a few seconds passed of complete quietness, she giggled at all the so-called hard legs who stood around her. "Now that you've boys showed me you're scared of the dark, how in the hell do we proceed with handling this so-called warfare?

Boom!

The loud explosion from underneath her feet rocked the ceiling roughly.

The guards wasted no time running headfirst out of the room to protect the household, and Torey shook his head with worry as he ran over to the window watching an assload of trucks slide up recklessly in the yard. "Looks like they bringing the party to you."

Frost cocked her pistol with joy as she heard the first semiautomatic sound off. "That's my cue." She smiled, walking out of the room with her gun aimed.

Eva was running down the hall with a panic and nearly tripped over her feet. "Frost, he's coming. They've found us!" She grabbed her hand with fear.

Pushing her arm away, Frost snapped, "No doubt, genius! I'm going to end this shit. Hopefully you're on the dance floor beside us." She kept her eyes focused on the hallway leading downstairs as the gunshots started to multiply

Pak, pak, pak, pak, pak!

Tat, tat, tat, tat, tat, tat, tat, tat!

Jamaican voices were yelling heavily in their patois language.

"Listen, we can let these crash outs handle this and leave, Frost. How can we be positive that we will win?" She shivered, ready to bail on the plan.

"Because, we always win. Now get the fuck out of my way, and if you're scared, hide in a fucking closet." Frost pushed past her, heading towards the catastrophe that was going on.

Running off for the office room where the meeting was just held, Eva looked around before stepping in and closing the door.

Chapter 20

After arriving at the secluded home, Ghost placed his team in position. Once the grenade sounded off, blowing the front door to pieces, he screamed through the walkie talkie radios that everyone was connected to. "Move in now!"

The trucks and SUV's swerved in front of the home with Ghost's men spilling out by the loads. Gunfire immediately erupted once his crew started to enter. After watching Tiffany, Laylah, Suave, and Stone break off to the right corridor of the home, Erica, along with himself, Shadow, and Sleeper, jumped from the vehicles like a trained military squad. Ghost led the pack, killing the first man who brushed out of the door way with his gun aimed. His P90 clapped, sending two slugs through his chest.

Erica caught the next victim as they spilled inside of the giant living room. He jumped from behind the hidden corridor and received a vicious blow to his throat. Grabbing a hold of his vest before he was able to fall, she placed her pistol to his brain, sending it across the tile floor. Sleeper and Shadow didn't hesitate to join in in the fun, slaughtering whatever they saw in their path as well.

"We taking the left side first!" Ghost yelled as he spotted the group of men pouring from the top level of the home.

Moving quickly as a team, they all slid down the long hallway with Sleeper airing out anything that moved behind them. The bullets were dancing off the walls and ceiling as if Iraq had waged war on the United States. The screaming voices mixing with the gunfire had him alert and prepared to kill whatever presented itself down at the end of the long hallway.

Watching a man jump out in front of him with a long 20 gauge pump, Ghost jumped at the barrel. He snatched it clean out of his hands and smashed the handle across his head.

Watching him fall to the floor, he started to beat him severely until the Jamaican's movements ceased. Aiming his P90 down at his body, he riddled him with a quick seven shots.

Pak! Pak! Pak! Pak! Pak! Pak! Pak!

The four of them entered a double door room at the end of the walkway. Sleeper slammed the doors shut and grabbed the giant lamp sitting directly next to the entrance. Breaking off the light fixture, he jammed it through the handles, barricading it off to slow a few of the men down.

A few more doors were connected to the room, but the empty section allowed them some borrowed time. Before Ghost could make a statement, the bullets started to erupt through the side windows, forcing them to drop down on the floor. The sound of a helicopter starting could be heard as the action sparked back up to a thousand degrees.

* * *

Sliding through the right corridor, Laylah eliminated the first three men with accurate shots to the head. Tiffany moved beside her, taking out the next goon who shot his pistol recklessly. Her gun popped four times, hitting him in the chest. She never got a chance to see the man directly behind because his first bullet popped, striking her in the right arm.

"Shit!" she cursed, nearly falling until Laylah reached back to grab a hold of her arm.

Suave didn't hesitate to blow a hole through the center of his throat as Stone stood at the bottom floor with his AK-47 clearing the pathway for when they made their way back down.

"I'm okay, I'm okay, baby girl." Tiffany gazed down at the flesh wound. She ripped off a piece of her shirt, tied it around her arm hastily, and continued up the stairs.

Frost could see them approaching and quickly fled the opposite way to slide down on the left side of her puzzle-style mansion. There were so many doors and exits that you would literally need X-ray goggles not to run into a henchmen that was gunning for your head.

They never caught sight of Frost, but Tiffany spotted Eva coming out of a room holding a medium-sized duffle bag once they reached the top of her stairs. She aimed her gun to shoot. She missed her by a small inch as the bitch headed up a flight of stairs, which looked like it was the attic.

"Keep pushing down until everything at the top is clear, baby girl. I'm going after her," she ordered before running after her.

Getting down to end of the hallway, she aimed her gun up the large staircase and began to climb quickly. The sound of the helicopter began to grow louder. Once she reached the top, she noticed the spacious attic with a window that was able to give the coward-ass old bitch a getaway. Jogging towards it, she aimed her gun, but it served no purpose. Eva was dashing across the top of their roof towards the chopper with a few bodyguards waiting for her. Tiffany closed one of her eyes, aiming the gun, and released four rapid shots. One found home in Eva's leg, forcing her to collapse. The men who stood in front of her quickly helped, pulling her inside the aircraft and then jumping in behind.

Watching the helicopter rise from the roof, she slammed a hand down on the window seal and headed back towards the attic stairs.

* * *

The war from the three large windows had Ghost, Shadow, and Sleeper popping their guns with no mercy. Half of the renegade Trenchtown Jamaicans were falling by the minute, and Ghost could tell that they were gaining victory from the sound of firepower coming from the other side of the home.

Erica sat behind them, so focused on reloading her weapon that she never saw the side door behind her slowly slide open. Shadow caught it at the last minute, and before he could say anything, Frost was aiming the sawed off shotgun at her back. "Erica, get down!"

Before she could react, Frost released a slug, blowing a giant hole through her back.

"Nooooo!" Ghost yelled with wide eyes. He reached out his arm as if she had snatched the soul from his body

Erica's face softened, and that's when he actually could see that humble, sweet woman he first met enter back in her system. Her gun dropped to the floor, and she managed to look up into Ghost's eyes. A small trail of blood trickled hastily down her lips. "I love you, baby," she murmured before receiving another bullet to the back, knocking her down.

Shadow instantly let loose his gun at the red devil as Ghost stood frozen in shock. The last shot she was able to get off struck him in the hip, sending him down to the floor before she backed out the side door, smoothly disappearing into the darkness.

Sleeper ran quickly over to Erica, scooping her up in his arms. Shadow turned around and executed the killer who tried to hop through the window with a bullet to the neck. Sleeper moved with Erica in his hands, kicking the glass loose and hopping out.

Shadow snatched the walkie talkie from his hip. "Tiffany, bail out. Get out the house now. We're hurt down here. Everybody out!"

Ghost's head was spinning like a merry go round, and before he could snap his eyes faded and he fell unconscious.

* * *

Courtney and Reeses are outside of the house with their eight man crew smoking everything in sight. A few of the killers came from the sides of the home and were taken out with ease. One of their trusted crew members caught the bad side of a slug and died directly beside them as they defended the front post to their best abilities. After watching the enemies subside, Courtney spotted Tiffany, Laylah, Suave, and Stone exit from the right side of the house with their guns still aimed for war. Only a few of their men were walking out of the mansion. A few were hit and bleeding profusely. Half were dead, and others who were truly built for a tragedy came out without a scratch.

Reeses was posted on the right side of the Infiniti truck, and nothing could stop her from running towards Sleeper and Shadow as they came slowly around the corner carrying Erica and dragging Ghost by his armpits. "What happened?" she screamed with a hand over mouth after seeing her family down bad.

"We gotta get them outta here." Sleeper's accent rang loudly as he rushed to put Erica inside of the truck. Shadow pulled Ghost to the car with his eyes roaming around for any enemies.

Tiffany and Laylah both sped across the parking lot until they reached the rest of the team.

"Oh my God, baby no, nooo, no!" she yelled, jumping in the backseat with Erica's dead body.

Laylah witnessed Ghost being placed into the backseat of the same truck. As the crew loaded up and started to swerve out of the mansion's driveway, she turned on her heels, heading running straight for the right side of Eva's hideout.

"Laylah!" Stone yelled as he watched her disappear behind the building.

Tiffany noticed that her daughter was breaking off on her own mission, and she refused to see her life taken in the process. As she tried to jump back out of the back seat, Shadow slammed the door.

"No. I'll get her. Get them out of here now! I got her. Just leave!" he ordered, rushing back towards the right side of the powerless home.

Instead of following her first mind, she obliged and remained in the backseat with both of her lovers lying gently against her. Ghost was sitting to the left side of her breathing erratically, but he was still unconscious, and Erica's lifeless body was stiff with her head laid across Tiffany's lap. Suave looked in the back, rubbing a hand across his sweaty face while staring at his best friend and sister. Tiffany's tears were pouring as she gazed up at him, shaking her head in disbelief. There would never be a day of resting if both the influential leaders of the family left them at that moment. It was past a devastating situation, and all he could do was pray that Shadow could at least make it back with Laylah as Sleeper took the front seat and mashed the pedal to the floor out of the secluded area.

Sitting in the darkness behind a large oak tree, Torey watched from afar smirking and quickly headed for his car that was parked on the other side of the thick woods.

* * *

Frost moved back through the top level of the home after slaying Erica and caught another one of their henchmen lying in the middle corridor that led to the other side of the mansion. He was wounded badly, dragging his body across the floor as if that would be sufficient enough to live. Slowly walking over to him with the sawed off shotgun aimed, her voice rattled his flesh.

"I'm sorry that I stumbled past you. Times up, sweetheart." She pulled the trigger, knocking his chest loose.

Letting the silence fill the air for a slight second, she exhaled and realized that Eva bailed out on her. The dirty scary cougar knew that she was more terrified to battle head to head with her father, but instead she led her to believe that the death of him was more than necessary. Her steps was already two steps ahead of the dumb bitch, and it was clear what she was trying to pull.

Frost walked into the meeting room and moved in quickly. She paced over to the giant office table, climbed on top of it, and reached up to remove the metal vent connected to the side wall. Letting it fall to the floor, she removed the laptop that sat inside. Hopping down and taking a seat at the table, she opened it up and placed the USB memory stick in the side. Clicking on a hidden file, she watched as all the offshore accounts popped rapidly on the screen. Each one was laced with at least two million dollars, and she didn't hesitate to start draining them into a private bank that she began to do business with on her own a few months back. It didn't take longer than three minutes, and the ten accounts Eva thought she was gonna run off with were emptier than a junkie's car rental. Grabbing the extra duffle that rested under the table, she placed the gun and laptop inside and prepared to leave the death-infested home.

Stepping back in the hallway, she froze in her tracks. Laylah was standing at the end of the top corridor. Her face was blank, and a seventeen shot Smith and Wesson handgun was dangling in her right hand.

Frost's eyes grew wide. She knew that her entire head could have been blown off, but instead of showing fear, she embraced the heart of her older sister and began to talk shit.

"I thought after our last encounter, I would never see you again."

Laylah didn't reply. She continued to remain quiet with tears of rage falling down her cheeks

"So I'm guessing you had your tongue blown out? Because I hate being ignored." Frost thought about the sawed-off shotgun she just placed inside the duffle. Her spare baby nine millimeter was strapped down to her leg. She didn't want to make a false move. Just when she started to think of an escape plan. Laylah tossed her gun to the floor, pulling a black stainless steel hunting knife from her side.

"Oooohhhh. Someone's up for a challenge." Frost tossed the bag to the side and cracked her neck from side to side. She slid a silver butcher blade from her side latch and took a step forward. Her mouth hung open as if she was drooling for blood. "Tonight you die!"

Their eyes didn't blink, and after a few seconds of silence, they both began to run towards each other. Frost swung her weapon towards her head, missing, as Laylah dodged it smoothly, landing a hard left fist into her jaw. The battle was on.

Shadow was creeping up the left side of the home, and happened to catch the action in full throttle. The two girls were going blow for blow with their deadly hands and their knives were moving faster than a fly dodging a swatter. Quickly stepping back behind the wall, he stared in amazement. Neither of them was trying to let up, and he couldn't get a clear shot at Frost while they were fighting for the kill.

164

Frost landed a kick to Laylah's side. She stumbled, but quickly regained her balance. Their knives were pointed out at one another like daggers aiming for a designated target. Both of their chests heaved with adrenaline, and Laylah still refused to let up. Swinging a roundhouse kick towards Frost's legs, she fell and rolled at the perfect time. Laylah's knife was coming down so fast that she sent small sparks flying across the concrete tile. Before she could rush back to her feet, she caught a vicious knee to the gut.

"Ugh!" Her face balled up in pain

She had enough energy to block Laylah's next one, which was aiming for the face, and still received an uppercut, forcing her knife to drop.

Laylah clutched her knife harder as she fell against the wall in a slight daze.

Shadow still remained behind the wall, but he never took his eyes off his sister's daughter.

Frost's nose was leaking profusely, and she could tell that the reaper was creeping down death's alley as her sister glared at her with malice. She was damn near seeing double from the hard knee and strike to the face, but she refused to quit.

"You can't beat me, Laylah. I can't lose!" she yelled before swinging a right haymaker.

Laylah ducked smoothly and jammed the large hunting knife up into the bottom of her chin, freezing the fight instantly. Frost's eyes glowed with pain, but she wasn't able to release anything but a small, shrill shriek. Yanking the knife out, Laylah kicked Frost violently in the face, forcing her soulless body to crash down on the cold floor.

Shadow's eyes grew wide as Laylah stood over Frost, plunging the blade back and forth into her neck. Blood covered her hands and Frost's body shook as Laylah started to sever her head from its shoulders. The sight alone forced his heart to beat uncontrollably. Not only did he know his niece was so fluent with her training, but he never knew that she had the same horrible traits as her father. He quickly made his way back down the steps. He knew that he had to ensure she got home, but it damn sure wasn't gonna be with him beside her.

Walking out of the house with his gun aimed, he jumped inside the last parked GMC truck and sat low in the seat. He could feel his chest quaking, and it was sad to say it, but a small paranoia moved through his body when he watched her walk out of the front door with Frost's head in her hand. She stood on the large porch with her knife in hand as if she was waiting for more competition. Dropping the blade, she gripped her stomach from the two deep wounds that were delivered from her sister's knife. Her mind was so locked in on taking Frost's life that she never felt the sharp metal pierce her.

Shadow watched as she moved across the spacious driveway over to Frost's parked 2019 BMW530. She deactivated the alarm using the keys she found in Frost's pocket. She climbed in the front seat and started the engine. Pulling hastily out of the parking lot, she made a right heading back for the boat dock.

Shadow started his engine right behind her, waiting until the headlights disappeared. He did the dash out of the driveway, making a smooth left heading for the shortcut to beat her from reaching the dock first. He hated to see her in so much pain, but he could at least guarantee the family one thing. One of the headaches that caused so much pain was damn sure suffering in the bottom of hell, and he wouldn't stop until he knew them all were six feet under for what they did to the woman he considered as his sister.

Chapter 21
The Grey mansion
One hour later

Feeling the needle prick his skin, Ghost grabbed the doctor's hand forcefully and sat up on the couch. His side instantly began to quake with an unbearable pain, causing Tiffany to rush over to him.

"Baby, calm down. I'm here." She placed a hand on his chest.

He stared into her emerald green eyes. He could tell that she had been crying for a long period of time. Rubbing her cheek, he stared around at everyone in the living room. Suave, Stone, and Reeses stood around with sad faces as if the world had just ended. Courtney was standing next to Sleeper by the staircase, and her head was hung low. The room was filled with silence, a little too much for Ghost.

"Where's Erica, Tiff?"

The question had her lips quivering, ready to drop another load of sorrow for the slain Queen. She could tell by the painful look on his face that he didn't really remember what had just occurred a few hours ago. Before she could reply, everybody's eyes cut towards Shadow as he stepped through the front door of the home by himself. He was speechless, and Tiffany's chest started to ache when she didn't spot her daughter behind him. Shadow walked over to her and Ghost with a hurt expression.

Tiffany stood up raising his head. "Please don't tell me anything bad," she said, ready to lose her mind if he didn't reply in time.

"Nah, sistas, nothing like that. She's safe. I just couldn't ride back with her. It's kind of hard for me to explain." He exhaled, not trying to make her panic.

"What do you mean?"

Ghost leaned his feet over the couch feeling that he was being left out on something. "I guess no one heard my question - unless I didn't really speak the shit out loud. Shadow, where's Erica, and where the fuck is my daughter?" His eyes were gazing up at his friend wanting an answer immediately.

Tiffany lowered her head, truly not wanting to be the one to give him the news after watching him suffer through so much earlier. She knew that Shadow was the best one to address the problem. She decided to trust his word about Laylah and stepped out of his way for him and Ghost to converse.

Shadow walked over and placed a hand on his friend's shoulder. "I think you need to get some rest before we try and have this conversation, dawg. I don't want you to spazz 'cause you're not in the best condition."

"Stop fucking around with me, bro. Tell me I was just dreaming. Tell me she isn't gone?" he questioned with a crackle in his voice, not wanting to accept the truth. His eyes slanted showing that his anger was starting to rise.

Knowing how furious his mind could get, Shadow refused to lie any longer. "I'm sorry, folk, but she's dead." He gave him a look of deep empathy.

Ghost's jaw clenched tightly, struggling to stand to his feet. He slowly walked over with tears forming in the corner of his eyes. "Bitch-ass nigga, I don't know what type of games you playing, but I suggest you cut the games, Shadow."

Shadow rubbed the bridge of his nose, letting the remark slide off his back, knowing that the truth was breaking his spirit. He allowed him to vent, but he refused to be the one to make him think that shit was peachy perfect. "Watch ya mouth, dawg. I'm only telling you the truth because I love ya, bro. You've been my brother since we were thirteen, and I've never hurt you once!" Shadow yelled. "She's gone, bro. I'm sorry."

Ghost closed his eyes tightly and tried to walk away from his friend. Shadow could see the pain in his face from the gunshot wound and tried to help him back to the couch. Ghost pushed his hand aggressively, causing himself to fall to the floor.

"Just get off me, man! I told you I didn't want to come back. I told you that every time I'm around, my family dies. I should've just stayed dead to everyone and she would still be here. Mariah would still be here!" he cried. You could feel the suffering that was cracking through his voice. He clasped his hands together. He looked to the sky as if he was Jesus asking why he had been forsaken. "I give up! I can't beat you, Lord. I'll submit, just please let this nightmare end for me. Please!" His hands were shaking from the news of his first beloved dying. Nothing could compare to the pain he felt at that exact moment.

Shadow couldn't take seeing his longtime friend so distressed. The bad part was he had forced Ghost to come back after he made the same statement about being a hex on the family. He never wanted to see anyone, especially close loved ones like Erica, being snatched away from him, and the guilt was truly eating at his heart. He walked off towards the patio and stepped out, closing it behind him.

No one could sit around watching the stress that Ghost was releasing, and everyone started to disperse out of respect for Tiffany's facial expression.

"He's not gonna properly heal if he doesn't rest, Ms. Grey," the doctor warned with a worried face.

"Just give me a second, please." She held up her hand.

Kneeling down beside her King, she wrapped a hand around his shoulder. She stared into his eyes. Their foreheads touched as they shared a short moment of silence. "Chance, I know that you're really hurting right now, and I can never say that you shouldn't, because I love her too. She was the strength of us. But that doesn't mean that we can let her down right now. If we give up, everyone else will give in, baby. Please don't let me down. I can't do this without you." She wiped the running streams from his face.

The sound of the front door opening forced them both to turn their heads at the same second. The sight of Laylah holding Frost's head forced both of their eyes to widen in shock. Blood was leaking slowly from the bottom of her bulletproof vest as she took a step across the threshold and fell face first to the floor.

"Laylah!" Tiffany yelled, running quickly to her side.

The doctor moved immediately over to them after noticing the hard fall she had taken. Ghost struggled to get to his feet, but fought through the pain in order to reach his little one. He couldn't help but to look down at his youngest daughter's head sitting gently on his floor. The sight of her red bloodshot eyes said that she suffered miserably before Laylah eliminated her from the earth.

Bending down slowly to touch his baby's forehead, he whispered in her ear as the doctor cut the vest slowly from her torso. "You can't die on me, baby girl. You did it. You're Daddy's true savage, and I've always believed in you. Just don't leave me." He kissed her delicately on the right cheek.

The team heard the small commotion of Tiffany begging her to wake up and started to make their way quickly back into the living room. Ghost ignored all other movements as he continued to brush her hair with his fingers gently. Enough torment was dealt, and he wasn't gonna be able to suffer the loss of another child. Chaos was moving throughout the house, and the karma for all the long past sins finally crashed upon their own land. All Ghost had left was the faith in the man above, and the rest of his living bloodline. There was never a time where he wanted to give it all up and settle for being average when it came to living the lifestyle he created for himself and the fam. After fast forwarding to that present time, he wished it all could just start back from the beginning, and it would all just be a bad dream.

Chris Green

Chapter 22
Downtown Kingston Hotel suites
24 hours later

It was around 10:47 p.m. when the woman stepped through the revolving glass door of the five star stay-in. Her black Versace zip up dress was fitting like a glove and her red Giuseppe heels clicked across the shiny tile floor. Her headache was kicking in big time, and a drink was surely needed before she took in for a closing tonight.

Making her way to the second floor bar, she stepped through the entrance and headed straight for the counter. The marble tabletop was loaded with a variety of bottled beverages, and the last open seat happened to catch her eyes. She climbed up on the barstool. She crossed her legs and tapped her fingernails gently on the glass.

"Excuse me, but can I have a Remy Martini with lime please?" She dug into her small handbag and slid a crispy Franklin across the bar top.

The middle-aged black Haitian man smiled, pulling a large glass from underneath the shelves. "Right away, ma'am." He turned around to retrieve her order.

Torey sat directly beside her with his eyes locked on her like she was a well done steak with a side of garlic cheese potatoes. She couldn't help but to laugh at his thirstiness, but it was still cute with him flashing that handsome ass smile. Instead of allowing him to lust, she spoke.

"Hi. It's not polite to stare," she said nonchalantly as if he was a local fan of her beauty.

"Says who? You really gonna sit here and tell me you ain't never gazed at that fine-ass woman in the mirror? I might lose the definition of everything if that's not polite." He admired her sexy aura and style.

Her caramel skin was the color of French vanilla coffee creamer. Her dreamy brown eyes added to the perfection, and her body was topping the last supermodel that landed on the *Maxim* cover edition.

"Thanks, but that's a creepy old man thing. Men who have mouths speak to women, not gaze." She showed him those pretty dimples as the bartender placed her drink down on the counter. Picking it up, she stirred the straw in a circle before taking a slow swig.

"Hmm," he mumbled thinking about how good she could work her lips for a tongue kiss. "So what brings you out here to Jamaica, baby? 'Cause you definitely a tourist. Where you from?"

"Jersey," she lied to see if he would bite the bait.

"I got a few people out in Jersey. I'm from Delaware, but I got a little Spanish side in me too. The top notch for sure. The name's Torey." He held out his hand, hoping she accepted.

Trying her best not to be stiff on him, she shook his hand gently. "Lia. And it's nice to meet you, Torey," she replied, looking him up, and down.

His Hugo boss peacoat set the tone with his tan Timberland boots. He wore a pair of Rag and Bone fitted jeans, and his hair was cut into a nice low temp fade. She could tell that whatever little money he came up on was treating him pretty decent. He wasn't a lame for sure, and she could see the handle of his gun every time he sat up straight to get a view of her face.

"So what are you doing in the islands alone? This isn't a dull place when it comes to women. You ain't caught you a baby mama yet?" She giggled.

"Nah. I'm actually leaving tomorrow. I had a delayed flight back up top. I decided to come get a room and just kick back for a few hours, and the night's still young. It's no telling who I might make a wifey."

"Oh, really?" She tooted up her lips at the weak-ass game he was running.

"Yeah, really. I'm saying, like if you not busy, you can come keep me company until I leave this little island. I just asked for the kitchen to bring me a few appetizer dishes upstairs, and I can't drink the two bottles of Ciroc I bought alone. I mean, if you not too busy to let a brother talk a few hours with you." Torey folded his arms as if he just knew she would accept.

"How the hell you know I ain't got a man sitting upstairs waiting for me already?" he shot back

"Because, he'd be down here dragging yo' fine ass up top with him. You would only have fifty seconds to get to the ice bucket and back before I came out to search for ya." Torey flashed his bright smile winning her over.

"Maybe a drink or two. But you don't have to try and butter me up. I'm single, and I'm warning you, I love to crack jokes, so please don't do no grown shit if you can't take the grown woman honesty," she warned, standing to her feet.

Torey huffed with a small chuckle, "I'm sure any response you give me will be a great one. I'm a wonderful guy," he bragged, walking smoothly beside her out of the open bar.

* * *

After reaching the luxurious suite, Torey made the beautiful lady feel right at home. He used the remote to rotate the curtains back where the city could glow up nicely. He poured up two glasses of peach Ciroc liquor and handed one to her.

"Thanks." She smiled, looking out of the large window.

The vibrant lights bounced gently across the sky showing the beautiful part of Jamaica. It was sad that she was never able to experience such things with her old lover now that she was able to do more than better for herself. Everything happened for a reason though, and regardless of how many hardships she suffered through, nothing would stop her from reaching self-happiness with dreams and life. Her mission would always be considered first, and nothing would be able to break that chain again after she made the personal promise.

"I've never met a woman so beautiful with a sense of humor like you. It's funny because you remind me of myself," Torey complimented her, taking a seat on the edge of the soft queen-sized mattress.

"I try. I don't like being dull, and I'm damn sure not a buzz kill. I love to live life to the fullest and be me. That's all I know." She shrugged before downing the first glass of liquor.

Seeing the mellow posture in her aura, Torey could tell that the drinks were definitely making her ease up real nice. He couldn't help but to stare at that petite ass every time she turned to glance back out the window. The hair on her head was lying straight down, and she would drag her fingers through it every time she gave a reply.

"Do you still feel like being honest if I do some grown man shit?" he asked, licking his lips, and grabbing ahold of his dick, showing the large prin.?

Rolling her eyes down to his package, she raised an eyebrow. The motherfucka definitely had something going on unless he had a pair of socks stuffed in his pants. Keeping her word as usual, she refused to be a different bitch. Setting the empty glass on his nightstand, she unzipped the side of her dress allowing it to hit the floor and then kicked her heels off. He looked at her banging-ass body in amazement.

"Damn!" His bottom lip was fidgeting as if he wanted to bite a chunk out of her.

The white Chanel lingerie set was showing off every curve, from the B-cup breasts to the smooth hips. She walked in front of him. She pushed him down on the bed, cradling his lap. He instantly reached down for her soft apple bottom, getting a nice squeeze.

"If that's what I think it is in yo' pants, then you might get a little honesty."

"I think I love you already, Lia." He leaned in slowly for a kiss.

Their lips intertwined passionately and once it broke, he felt the thin sharp razor glide smoothly across his throat. He shot his hands straight up to the nasty, deep wound. Blood began to pour profusely from his neck.

The woman looked at him, staring deeply into his pupils. She smiled. "You don't remember me, do you, Torey? Take a good, hard look, baby boy. Hard as that big dick that's turning soft in your pants right now. Or maybe you remember my child's father, Ryan?"

Torey eyes were wide as he gargled on his own blood. The light was fading quickly, but the sight of her beautiful face was still visible as he struggled to stay on God's green earth.

"You took him away from me, when that was supposed to have been my job. You touched a dead man, and that soul has to now be replaced with yours. So bleed, Torey, bleed out," she said with a deranged look before leaning down to kiss his shivering lips.

Before she could stand to her feet, he was inhaling and taking his last breath. Calmly placing back on her designer dress, she scooted his leg over to take a seat while placing her heels back on. Exhaling a sigh of relief, she got up and gazed back down at his dead body.

"Goodbye, darling."
Faith, the Black Widow, grabbed one of the bottles of Ciroc and turned out the lights before exiting the hotel room.

Chapter 23
The Grey mansion
Three days later

The bright blue sky shined in Ghost's eyes as he stepped out on his small field of grass that rested behind the home. Knowing that there was only so much space, he had a nice crew place a large sepulcher over the two tombstones that had been planted the night before.

Walking slowly over, he knelt down, gazing at them both. *Erica, great loving mother, wife, and leader* was engraved on one with a pair of prayer hands, and *Mariah, great dedicated daughter, sister, and princess that was a blessing to be a part of the family* was on the opposite. The two loves were a string that twirled the lining out of his heart, but he knew that God's plan had to be successful if he wanted the outcome of his turmoil to change. There wasn't a minute that passed where he didn't think of them, and that alone let him know he was building for the better to ensure that he caused no more mistakes for the near future. Eva and Torey, the young nephew he recently discovered, were the last two missing pieces of the drama, and the word alone was gonna have them running for their entire lives unless they placed a gun to each other's temple and pulled the trigger. Revenge for his Queen and Princess was surely gonna be upheld by any means. The thought of his big brother flashed in his mind. Even Bernard and his mother. All of them were now resting in a better place, but would never be forgotten.

"Baby, Courtney's asking for you. Her ride to the airport is ready, and Shadow is here." Tiffany peeped her head out the patio door.

Blowing a kiss at his two resting love bugs, he headed back inside.

Laylah was resting on a couch in a pair of black Nike pajamas. Her face brightened like the sun when he stepped inside.

"Hey Daddy!"

"Wassup, pumpkin? I see you finally woke up. You couldn't even stay up and taste the dessert I made last night. How you feel?" he asked, kissing her forehead.

"I feel better, Daddy. I miss them, but I'm better." She nodded with assurance.

"That's my baby." He smiled, rubbing a hand through her silky hair.

Shadow walked inside of the living room with a sly grin on his face. "I need to holla at you, bro. You wouldn't believe what I found out."

"Cool. Give me one second to holler at Courtney, and I'll be right back." He jogged smoothly through the small hallway until he reached the front door where she was standing. Her bags was sitting on the floor beside her, and all she could do was twiddle with her fingers when he approached. "Wassup, kiddo?"

"Hey Ghost. I just wanted to thank you personally for accepting me to fight along the side of your family. It was an honor. I'm not sure where I'm heading now, but the money you gave me will be used wisely. I'll never forget you guys," she said sincerely

"We won't either, Courtney, and thank you for keeping your loyalty through all the bull."

Nodding, she picked up her bags and pondered on something else to buy some time. "Uhhh, I don't think I gave you all my info just in case you may ever need me." Courtney set the bags back down to search for a pen.

Grabbing her arm, Ghost looked at her with a caring face. "You don't have to go if you don't want to, Courtney. We have more than enough room."

"Oh no, Ghost. I couldn't possibly intrude on you guys like that. I mean, you already have so many family members to look out for and——"

"Girl, do yo' ass wanna stay or not? It ain't nothing but some international criminals all around this home, if you ain't noticed," Tiffany cut her off with a huge smile. All she could see in her was another needy Erica, and that's just what she felt they needed. A new presence.

Courtney smiled in disbelief. "Oh my God! This is so unreal. I've never had real friends like you guys, and I would be honored to stay."

Ghost dragged her bags quickly back into the living room, and pulled Tiffany in for a hug.

Ghost laughed while shaking his head knowing that the crew couldn't get any bigger, or crazier. It was a part of their tradition. Taking in the loyal, and getting rid of the deceitful.

He allowed the girls to converse while he moved towards Shadow who sat at the dining room table typing on his laptop. "What's the lick read, brudda?" he asked, taking a seat beside him.

"A lot. Do you remember the body that was found inside the Kingston Hotel in Jamaica a few days ago? A few of our resources say that it happened to be ya sneaky nephew who caught that vicious slice to the neck. You know the media released his name. 'Nineteen-year-old Torey Ramirez was found dead in the room of his hotel suite in the Kingston Hotel' is what the media pushing in the papers. I slid down to the address myself. I had a little talk with the head of security, and he gave a small gift for a little fee - on behalf of Erica and

General Cannon helping him build the business that he's running today."

"What's that?" Ghost's eyes glared at him curiously.

"We got the security camera from his hallway," he answered, pulling up the recordings for that entire night. He fast forwarded past the part where the woman entered the room with him. He paused it quickly when she walked out of the room by herself with a bottle of liquor in hand. Her face was still wearing the evil smile, and Ghost was trying his best to recognize her as he stared at the screen.

"Who the fuck is she?"

"That's the part where I'm lost at, folk. She has to be somebody, taking your little problem out of the game with ease like that. With Eva still running around, there's never no telling who she could be getting rid of."

"Hmm." Ghost smirked, staring at the computer. "I don't give a fuck who she works for. Send somebody to find her. It don't matter what it cost," he ordered.

"You know I'm in on it, dawg." He dug in his pocket, pulling out his touchscreen.

The sound of a distant helicopter hovering over Ghost's home forced him to grab his gun from the counter and move towards the back patio. Shadow, Laylah, and even Tiffany did the same.

He stepped back out into the blazing sun. The chopper was landing down at the bottom of his beach, and he could see over fifteen men jumping off with FBI jackets on their backs. Two small boats with a twenty man military crew were pulling up to the shore, and they all wasted no time jumping out before touching the sand to get a rush on the family home.

Ghost didn't run, nor did the family as they stood behind him firmly. Suave and Stone were woken out of bed by Courtney, and they wasted no time falling out of the home with their assault rifles in hand.

The leading agent held a piece of paper up as he reached the bottom stairs of Ghost's mansion. They stood at least forty feet back from the notorious family as he removed his shades.

"Chance Grey? I'm Kenny Washington, FBI, and you're under arrest for being a wanted fugitive in the United States, along with all the others behind you," he stated with his men pointing their weapons

Ghost laughed with his head down. He knew that one day the people would finally come, but that life he lived was no longer a part of him, so placing a pair of cuffs on for the past deeds was definitely out of the question. "I'm sorry, sir, I mean no disrespect, but I'm just a normal guy now. I'm not living the life of crime any longer, and the people wouldn't allow you to do that unless you blow up this entire island," he responded calmly.

"The only people making the rules are me and the bullets that are in my damn soldiers' guns, son."

The sound of loud cars speeding and sliding into his front parking lot caused the men to point their guns recklessly. Over seventeen of Ghost's new crew members began to aim their assault rifles over the roof of his home, placing a beam directly on the talkative man's forehead. The rest began to pour behind the home with their straps aimed, prepared to die for the man who gave them another chance at life. There was no such thing as having to worry about any more problems when the entire island considered you king.

The large group of men was a small army, too many guns, and people to have an all-out battle in his backyard. The red beam slid down to the agent's chest, forcing him to breathe a little harder.

Ghost exhaled before folding his arms. "As I said, sir, I'm out of that life, but I also have a new family to feed. I don't think that they can respect the wishes that you're requesting, but it's all up to you." He smiled.

Taking a small step back, Agent Washington forced his men to lower their guns. He knew for a fact that it was suicide to even release a warning shot, and he refused to see a bunch of innocent men die for the cause of one person. "I'll be seeing you're around, Mr. Grey." He placed his shades on and turned around to head back down the beach.

Ghost's soldiers started to cheer loudly as they watched the crooked government workers climb back on the helicopter and boats retreating from the property. The looks on their faces said more than that they won. It said that they were happy. The loved ones stood behind him with huge smirks, and truly that was what it was all about: happiness.

"Thank you, baby." He looked up into the sky before turning around to head back in the crib. "Who wanna barbeque? '' he yelled, watching everyone break off for the house.

He knew that his crew were more than family and friends. They were real True Savages. Ones that could never be replaced.

Chapter 23
Wilmington, Delaware, 4:30 p.m.

Pulling up in her new Black Lexus coupe, Eva stepped out and headed up the porch of the nice home. Her hair was wrapped in a bun, and a mink coat was draped over her back. The Dior dress and heels on her feet added to her designer outfit perfectly, and she removed her Dolce and Gabbana shades before knocking on the door.

It didn't take but a few seconds for Free to open it, looking her up and down. "What do you want? Ryan ain't here, Ms. Lady."

"I'm not looking for Ryan. I'm here for you."

Giving her a weird look, he opened the door wider. "What the hell you want with me?"

"Allow me to step in and clarify. Do you have something to drink?"

Flashing a sly smile, he stepped to the side. "Hell yeah. Whatever you want!" He stepped to the side, letting her in before closing the door behind them.

To Be Continued...
True Savage 8
Coming Soon

Submission Guideline

Submit the first three chapters of your completed manuscript to ldpsubmissions@gmail.com, subject line: Your book's title. The manuscript must be in a .doc file and sent as an attachment. Document should be in Times New Roman, double spaced and in size 12 font. Also, provide your synopsis and full contact information. If sending multiple submissions, they must each be in a separate email.

Have a story but no way to send it electronically? You can still submit to LDP/Ca$h Presents. Send in the first three chapters, written or typed, of your completed manuscript to:

LDP: Submissions Dept
Po Box 944
Stockbridge, Ga 30281

DO NOT send original manuscript. Must be a duplicate.

Provide your synopsis and a cover letter containing your full contact information.

Thanks for considering LDP and Ca$h Presents.

Coming Soon from Lock Down Publications/Ca$h Presents

BOW DOWN TO MY GANGSTA

By **Ca$h**

TORN BETWEEN TWO

By **Coffee**

THE STREETS STAINED MY SOUL **II**

By **Marcellus Allen**

BLOOD OF A BOSS **VI**

SHADOWS OF THE GAME II

By **Askari**

LOYAL TO THE GAME **IV**

By **T.J. & Jelissa**

IF LOVING YOU IS WRONG… **III**

By **Jelissa**

TRUE SAVAGE **VIII**

MIDNIGHT CARTEL III

DOPE BOY MAGIC IV

CITY OF KINGZ II

By **Chris Green**

BLAST FOR ME **III**

A SAVAGE DOPEBOY III

CUTTHROAT MAFIA III

DUFFLE BAG CARTEL VI

By **Ghost**

A HUSTLER'S DECEIT III

KILL ZONE **II**

Chris Green

BAE BELONGS TO ME III
A DOPE BOY'S QUEEN III
By **Aryanna**
COKE KINGS V
KING OF THE TRAP II
By **T.J. Edwards**
GORILLAZ IN THE BAY V
3X KRAZY II
De'Kari
THE STREETS ARE CALLING II
Duquie Wilson
KINGPIN KILLAZ IV
STREET KINGS III
PAID IN BLOOD III
CARTEL KILLAZ IV
DOPE GODS III
Hood Rich
SINS OF A HUSTLA II
ASAD
KINGZ OF THE GAME VI
Playa Ray
SLAUGHTER GANG IV
RUTHLESS HEART IV
By Willie Slaughter
THE HEART OF A SAVAGE III
By Jibril Williams
FUK SHYT II

By Blakk Diamond

THE REALEST KILLAZ III

By Tranay Adams

TRAP GOD III

By Troublesome

YAYO IV

GHOST MOB

Stilloan Robinson

KINGPIN DREAMS III

By Paper Boi Rari

CREAM II

By Yolanda Moore

SON OF A DOPE FIEND III

By Renta

FOREVER GANGSTA II

GLOCKS ON SATIN SHEETS III

By Adrian Dulan

LOYALTY AIN'T PROMISED III

By Keith Williams

THE PRICE YOU PAY FOR LOVE II

By Destiny Skai

CONFESSIONS OF A GANGSTA III

By Nicholas Lock

I'M NOTHING WITHOUT HIS LOVE II

SINS OF A THUG II

By Monet Dragun

LIFE OF A SAVAGE IV

Chris Green

MURDA SEASON IV

GANGLAND CARTEL III

By **Romell Tukes**

QUIET MONEY IV

THUG LIFE II

By **Trai'Quan**

THE STREETS MADE ME III

By **Larry D. Wright**

THE ULTIMATE SACRIFICE VI

IF YOU CROSS ME ONCE II

ANGEL III

By **Anthony Fields**

FRIEND OR FOE III

By **Mimi**

SAVAGE STORMS II

By **Meesha**

BLOOD ON THE MONEY II

By J-Blunt

THE STREETS WILL NEVER CLOSE II

By K'ajji

NIGHTMARES OF A HUSTLA II

By King Dream

THE WIFEY I USED TO BE II

By Nicole Goosby

IN THE ARM OF HIS BOSS

By Jamila

<u>Available Now</u>

RESTRAINING ORDER **I & II**

By **CA$H & Coffee**

LOVE KNOWS NO BOUNDARIES **I II & III**

By **Coffee**

RAISED AS A GOON I, II, III & IV

BRED BY THE SLUMS I, II, III

BLAST FOR ME I & II

ROTTEN TO THE CORE I II III

A BRONX TALE I, II, III

DUFFLE BAG CARTEL I II III IV V

HEARTLESS GOON I II III IV

A SAVAGE DOPEBOY I II

HEARTLESS GOON I II III

DRUG LORDS I II III

CUTTHROAT MAFIA I II

By **Ghost**

LAY IT DOWN **I & II**

LAST OF A DYING BREED

BLOOD STAINS OF A SHOTTA I & II III

By **Jamaica**

LOYAL TO THE GAME I II III

LIFE OF SIN I, II III

By **TJ & Jelissa**

BLOODY COMMAS I & II

SKI MASK CARTEL I II & III

Chris Green

KING OF NEW YORK I II,III IV V
RISE TO POWER I II III
COKE KINGS I II III IV
BORN HEARTLESS I II III IV
KING OF THE TRAP
By **T.J. Edwards**
IF LOVING HIM IS WRONG…I & II
LOVE ME EVEN WHEN IT HURTS I II III
By **Jelissa**
WHEN THE STREETS CLAP BACK I & II III
THE HEART OF A SAVAGE I II
By **Jibril Williams**
A DISTINGUISHED THUG STOLE MY HEART I II & III
LOVE SHOULDN'T HURT I II III IV
RENEGADE BOYS I II III IV
PAID IN KARMA I II III
SAVAGE STORMS
By **Meesha**
A GANGSTER'S CODE I &, II III
A GANGSTER'S SYN I II III
THE SAVAGE LIFE I II III
CHAINED TO THE STREETS I II III
BLOOD ON THE MONEY
By J-Blunt
PUSH IT TO THE LIMIT
By **Bre' Hayes**
BLOOD OF A BOSS **I, II, III, IV, V**

192

SHADOWS OF THE GAME

By **Askari**

THE STREETS BLEED MURDER **I, II & III**

THE HEART OF A GANGSTA I II& III

By **Jerry Jackson**

CUM FOR ME I II III IV V VI

An **LDP Erotica Collaboration**

BRIDE OF A HUSTLA **I II & II**

THE FETTI GIRLS **I, II& III**

CORRUPTED BY A GANGSTA I, II III, IV

BLINDED BY HIS LOVE

THE PRICE YOU PAY FOR LOVE

DOPE GIRL MAGIC I II III

By **Destiny Skai**

WHEN A GOOD GIRL GOES BAD

By **Adrienne**

THE COST OF LOYALTY I II III

By Kweli

A GANGSTER'S REVENGE **I II III & IV**

THE BOSS MAN'S DAUGHTERS I II III IV V

A SAVAGE LOVE **I & II**

BAE BELONGS TO ME I II

A HUSTLER'S DECEIT I, II, III

WHAT BAD BITCHES DO I, II, III

SOUL OF A MONSTER I II III

KILL ZONE

A DOPE BOY'S QUEEN I II

Chris Green

By **Aryanna**
A KINGPIN'S AMBITON
A KINGPIN'S AMBITION **II**
I MURDER FOR THE DOUGH
By **Ambitious**
TRUE SAVAGE I II III IV V VI VII
DOPE BOY MAGIC I, II, III
MIDNIGHT CARTEL I II
CITY OF KINGZ
By **Chris Green**
A DOPEBOY'S PRAYER
By **Eddie "Wolf" Lee**
THE KING CARTEL **I, II & III**
By **Frank Gresham**
THESE NIGGAS AIN'T LOYAL **I, II & III**
By **Nikki Tee**
GANGSTA SHYT **I II &III**
By **CATO**
THE ULTIMATE BETRAYAL
By **Phoenix**
BOSS'N UP **I , II & III**
By **Royal Nicole**
I LOVE YOU TO DEATH
By Destiny J
I RIDE FOR MY HITTA
I STILL RIDE FOR MY HITTA
By **Misty Holt**

LOVE & CHASIN' PAPER

By **Qay Crockett**

TO DIE IN VAIN

SINS OF A HUSTLA

By **ASAD**

BROOKLYN HUSTLAZ

By **Boogsy Morina**

BROOKLYN ON LOCK I & II

By **Sonovia**

GANGSTA CITY

By **Teddy Duke**

A DRUG KING AND HIS DIAMOND I & II III

A DOPEMAN'S RICHES

HER MAN, MINE'S TOO I, II

CASH MONEY HO'S

THE WIFEY I USED TO BE

By Nicole Goosby

TRAPHOUSE KING **I II & III**

KINGPIN KILLAZ I II III

STREET KINGS I II

PAID IN BLOOD **I II**

CARTEL KILLAZ I II III

DOPE GODS I II

By **Hood Rich**

LIPSTICK KILLAH **I, II, III**

CRIME OF PASSION I II & III

FRIEND OR FOE I II

By **Mimi**

STEADY MOBBN' **I, II, III**

THE STREETS STAINED MY SOUL

By **Marcellus Allen**

WHO SHOT YA **I, II, III**

SON OF A DOPE FIEND I II

Renta

GORILLAZ IN THE BAY **I II III IV**

TEARS OF A GANGSTA I II

3X KRAZY

DE'KARI

TRIGGADALE I II III

Elijah R. Freeman

GOD BLESS THE TRAPPERS I, II, III

THESE SCANDALOUS STREETS I, II, III

FEAR MY GANGSTA I, II, III IV, V

THESE STREETS DON'T LOVE NOBODY I, II

BURY ME A G I, II, III, IV, V

A GANGSTA'S EMPIRE I, II, III, IV

THE DOPEMAN'S BODYGAURD I II

THE REALEST KILLAZ I II

Tranay Adams

THE STREETS ARE CALLING

Duquie Wilson

MARRIED TO A BOSS... I II III

By Destiny Skai & Chris Green

KINGZ OF THE GAME I II III IV V

Playa Ray

SLAUGHTER GANG I II III

RUTHLESS HEART I II III

By Willie Slaughter

FUK SHYT

By Blakk Diamond

DON'T F#CK WITH MY HEART I II

By Linnea

ADDICTED TO THE DRAMA I II III

IN THE ARM OF HIS BOSS II

By Jamila

YAYO I II III

A SHOOTER'S AMBITION I II

By S. Allen

TRAP GOD I II

By Troublesome

FOREVER GANGSTA

GLOCKS ON SATIN SHEETS I II

By Adrian Dulan

TOE TAGZ I II III

By Ah'Million

KINGPIN DREAMS I II

By Paper Boi Rari

CONFESSIONS OF A GANGSTA I II

By Nicholas Lock

I'M NOTHING WITHOUT HIS LOVE

SINS OF A THUG

By Monet Dragun
CAUGHT UP IN THE LIFE I II III
By Robert Baptiste
NEW TO THE GAME I II III
By **Malik D. Rice**
LIFE OF A SAVAGE I II III
A GANGSTA'S QUR'AN I II III
MURDA SEASON I II III
GANGLAND CARTEL I II
By **Romell Tukes**
LOYALTY AIN'T PROMISED I II
By Keith Williams
QUIET MONEY I II III
THUG LIFE
By **Trai'Quan**
THE STREETS MADE ME I II
By **Larry D. Wright**
THE ULTIMATE SACRIFICE I, II, III, IV, V
KHADIFI
IF YOU CROSS ME ONCE
ANGEL I II
By **Anthony Fields**
THE LIFE OF A HOOD STAR
By Ca$h & Rashia Wilson
THE STREETS WILL NEVER CLOSE
By K'ajji
CREAM

True Savage 7

By Yolanda Moore

NIGHTMARES OF A HUSTLA

By King Dream

Chris Green

<u>BOOKS BY LDP'S CEO, CA$H</u>

<u>TRUST IN NO MAN</u>

<u>TRUST IN NO MAN 2</u>

<u>TRUST IN NO MAN 3</u>

<u>BONDED BY BLOOD</u>

<u>SHORTY GOT A THUG</u>

<u>THUGS CRY</u>

<u>THUGS CRY 2</u>

<u>THUGS CRY 3</u>

<u>TRUST NO BITCH</u>

<u>TRUST NO BITCH 2</u>

<u>TRUST NO BITCH 3</u>

<u>TIL MY CASKET DROPS</u>

<u>RESTRAINING ORDER</u>

<u>RESTRAINING ORDER 2</u>

<u>IN LOVE WITH A CONVICT</u>

<u>LIFE OF A HOOD STAR</u>

True Savage 7